REVENGE IN RED SPRINGS

by

Jim Bowden

Dales Large Print Books
Long Preston, North Yorkshire,
BD23 4ND, England.

British Library Cataloguing in Publication Data.

Bowden, Jim
    Revenge in Red Springs.

    A catalogue record of this book is
    available from the British Library

    ISBN   978-1-84262-700-6 pbk

First published in Great Britain in 1962 by Robert Hale Ltd.

Copyright © Jim Bowden 1962

Cover illustration © Gordon Crabb

Published in Large Print 2011 by arrangement with
Mr W. D. Spence

Dales Large Print is an imprint of Library Magna Books Ltd.

Printed and bound in Great Britain by
T.J. (International) Ltd., Cornwall, PL28 8RW

Chapter One

'Thet hombre's not gettin' away with it; we'll ride straight in an' shoot the place up!'

Lee Brown spat angrily. The short, thick-set man ran his broad fingers through his thick, black hair as he paced up and down. His dark-brown eyes smouldered with hate. He stopped, picked up a log, and threw it on to the fire, making the hot embers flare and light up the faces of his two brothers who sat near the flames trying to find some warmth on this chill night in the heart of the Wichita Mountains in southern Oklahoma.

'Calm down, Lee,' said Ed. 'Wes was killed three years ago.'

'Thet doesn't matter,' snarled Lee, spinning round to face his tall, slim brother. 'We must avenge his killin'. I know we hadn't seen Wes fer a number of years, but he was our brother, an' we can't let a two-bit tin-star get away with shootin' Wes.'

Ed looked hard at Lee. His hawk-like eyes searched the dark, unshaven, angry face, grimly lit by the dancing flames. 'Lee,' said

7

Ed quietly but firmly, 'I'm boss of this outfit an' we'll do things my way, an' I say we'll wait.'

Lee scowled. 'What's this,' he mocked, 'the great Ed Brown goin' soft?'

Ed tensed himself as Lee's words cut into his brain. His eyes narrowed, and his jaw tightened. He knew Lee to be hot-headed, but he also realised that to quarrel amongst themselves could be fatal to the biggest outlaw gang in Oklahoma. He controlled the urge to leap to his feet and smash Lee's words down his throat.

'You know thet'll never happen,' hissed Ed grimly. 'I never said we wouldn't avenge Wes, but as fer ridin' hell fer leather into Red Springs to git this here Dan McCoy – wal thet's the right way to commit suicide.'

Lee grunted and sat down cross-legged on the opposite side of the fire to his brothers. 'Wal, git on with it; what's your idea?' he said.

'Make McCoy squirm,' replied Ed. 'Make him really pay.'

'Bah!' snapped Lee who preferred action to drawn-out schemes. 'What's thet matter so long as we git him? What's your idea, Nick?' He looked sharply at his brother, who so far had said nothing about Wes' death.

8

The broad-shouldered, clean-shaven man leaned back on his arms and stretched his legs towards the fire. His fair hair was in marked contrast to that of his two darker brothers. A faint smile played around his lips and he glanced from one to the other before he spoke.

'Wal,' he drawled, 'I reckon you're both plumb crazy. What's the use of breakin' our nice set-up here jest to kill a sheriff in some hick town in Texas?'

'You've a point there, Nick,' agreed Ed. 'It may be better to stay here.'

'What's the matter with you two?' Lee snapped disgustedly. 'If we take the whole outfit with us we could blast the town apart.'

'Shore, shore,' agreed Nick. 'An' thet would ruin our set-up here fer certain.'

'Wal, let us three go,' pressed Lee. 'It won't do the boys any harm to be left on their own fer a while.'

'I'm not so sure,' answered Ed, rubbing his chin thoughtfully. 'They're liable to git restless, maybe break out on their own an' without our organisation thet would ruin everythin'.'

'But we aren't goin' to let this tin-star git away with it, even if Wes was on the wrong side of the law,' urged Lee.

9

'Wes was always the lone wolf,' pointed out Nick. 'We hadn't seen him fer years; been different if he'd been with us, one of the gang.'

'He's your brother!' yelled Lee pushing himself to his feet. He glared fiercely across the flickering flames at Nick. Anger flared inside him at the way his brother appeared to have taken the news so calmly.

'Lee, calm down,' said Nick quietly. 'I'm not sayin' we should forget this here McCoy altogether, but let's leave it fer the time being. We can catch up with him whenever we want; what's a bit longer matter? The news of Wes' death has taken considerable time to reach us, an' after all, this set-up here is bringin' in good dividends. What do you say, Ed?'

The tall, lean man, stared at the fire for a moment before pushing himself to his feet.

'Nick has a point,' he agreed, 'and there are several jobs coming up which we could pull. I reckon we should see them through first an' then reconsider headin' fer Red Springs.'

'Bah!' Lee spat into the hot embers. 'We should ride now, an' ride fast,' stormed the short, thick-set man. 'There'll always be jobs croppin' up an' we'll never ride to Texas. I reckon I'll hev to ride alone.'

Ed stared hard at his brother. 'Don't do anythin' foolish,' he warned. 'Some day we'll git McCoy, but not now.' Ed patted Lee on the arm. 'I know how you feel, but give it until daylight.'

Lee pulled his arm sharply away from Ed, spun on his heel, and hurried away from the fire.

The two older brothers watched him cross the hollow, climb amongst some rocks, and, silhouetted against the night sky, sit down to stare moodily across the Wichita Mountains.

Ed watched him for a while. He did not want to lose his brother for the jobs on hand. Lee was tough, quick with a gun, and he always seemed to be on the spot when needed.

Ed sat down staring unseeingly at the fire, recalling how the three brothers had moved westwards gathering around them men on the wrong side of the law, and youngsters who, searching for adventure, threw in their lot with the Browns to find that before long they could never take their place in a decent community again. Missouri, Kansas, and Colorado, had all felt the fury of the Brown gang before they turned south-east, back into Oklahoma, to establish themselves in the Wichita Mountains. Ed had seen great potential in this area and had split his gang into four groups, one to operate on each side of the mountains, whilst the three brothers moved throughout the entire region organising the raids and hold-ups.

Lee stared moodily in the darkness. To his right the light from the flickering flames danced across the reclining forms of his two brothers. He might have known they would not feel the same way about Wes as he did. Wes had been his boyhood companion, and why he had drifted away from them Lee never really knew. Anger smouldered in his eyes as he thought of his brother's death at the hands of a Texas lawman. He pulled his Colt from his holster, toying with it, as he stared over the Wichita Mountains, over which the pale moon was beginning to cast its eerie glow.

Suddenly, he slammed his Colt back into its holster and jumped to his feet. He hurried towards the camp but slowed as he neared the sleeping figures and crept quietly past them to his own saddle and bedroll. Lee picked up his belongings and moved silently to his horse which he comforted with soft words. When all was ready, Lee gathered some stones together and formed them into letters close to his brothers' horses. He glanced at the sleeping forms, hurried to his horse, and led it quietly away from the camp. After he had gone a quarter of a mile he climbed into the saddle and kept the animal at a walking pace for another half mile before turning it down the hillside and putting it into a trot. He kept to a steady pace heading in a southerly direction.

After five miles he saw the faint flicker of a camp fire a short distance ahead.

The clop of the horse's hoofs on the hard ground brought a cry of 'Hold it! Who's there?'

Lee pulled the horse to a halt knowing that somewhere in the darkness the sights of a rifle were trained on him.

'It's Lee,' he called.

'All right, come forward,' came the reply.

Lee pushed his horse towards the camp and was soon swinging from the saddle as several cowboys rolled themselves out of their blankets wondering what brought Lee to their camp at this time of night.

'Howdy, Lee,' greeted a dark, swarthy, moustached man. 'Strange time to come callin'; must hev a big raid planned?'

'No, Wally,' replied Lee, 'somethin' a bit

13

different which I've planned myself.'

Wally glanced sharply at Lee, and the other men moved closer wondering at this unusual deviation from the normal running of the gang.

Lee quickly explained the purpose of his ride to Red Springs. 'I want five of you to ride with me,' he concluded. 'The other one has to ride to Ed at daylight, not before. I left a message but he won't know I've taken any of you with me, so tell him just what I've done.'

He signalled out the five men he wanted, instructed them to saddle their horses and before long six men were riding steadily away from the Wichita Mountains towards the State of Texas.

The warming rays of the morning sun slid over the edge of the hillside and flooded the hollow with the light of a new day. Ed stirred in his blankets, blinked his eyes at the brightness and stretched himself. He glanced at the still, sleeping form of Nick but was startled when he saw no one occupied the position usually taken by Lee. He sat up and glanced at the rock on which he had last seen Lee, but no one was there.

Ed flung the blankets to one side and

sprang to his feet. He looked around the hollow, but here was no sign of his younger brother. Suddenly he stiffened. There were only two horses across the hollow.

'Nick! Nick!' shouted Ed. 'Wake up. Lee's gone!' He bent over his brother, shook him roughly, and pulled the blankets off him.

Nick groaned and rolled over. 'What's the matter?' he slurred sleepily.

'Lee's gone!' replied Ed emphatically.

Nick sat up slowly, rubbing his eyes. The words suddenly penetrated his brain. He stared unbelievingly at Ed.

'Horse, saddle, bedroll, the lot gone,' insisted Ed.

Nick was soon on his feet beside his brother and the two men hurried towards their horses hoping to find some trail left by Lee. As they neared the animals Nick suddenly grasped Ed's arm, halting him in his tracks. He pointed at the stones left by Lee on which they had almost trodden without noticing them.

'What the...?' gasped Ed, staring at the crude letters spelt out by the stones.

'Wes!' read Nick, surprise in his voice. He turned to Ed to see anger flashing in his eyes.

'The young fool,' stormed Ed. 'Why didn't

15

he wait until morning?'

'We can go after him,' suggested Nick.

'What's the use, he'll be miles away by now,' replied Ed kicking viciously at the stones. 'I wanted him here, this leaves us a good gun short.'

'He must be headin' fer Red Springs,' said Nick. 'Maybe we can catch him an' bring him back, or ride on with him.'

Ed glanced sharply at Nick. 'You wantin' to go now?' he snapped. 'I told him to leave revenge until later. Wal, as far as I'm concerned thet's how it stays. Lee can take his chances: if he pulls it off it'll save us a job: if not – wal thet's too bad, an' it'll be two killin's fer us to avenge.' He swung sharply on his heel and hurried towards the fire. 'C'm on, let's have some breakfast,' he called over his shoulder.

They soon had the fire blazing and were enjoying the food when the beat of hoofs caught their attention. The two men looked questioningly at each other, put down their plates, climbed slowly to their feet and drew their Colts.

'May be Lee,' whispered Nick, but his hopes were dashed when he saw that it was not his brother who broke the sky-line and rode down into the hollow.

'Mart Webster,' gasped Ed, surprised to see this man riding to their camp. 'How did he know where to find us?'

The two men holstered their Colts and awaited the arrival of Webster.

'Howdy, Ed; howdy, Nick,' greeted the newcomer as he swung from the saddle in front of the two brothers.

'What brings you here, Mart?' asked Ed.

'Lee told me where to find you,' answered Mart. 'Said I was to ride to you at day-break an' tell you thet he's taken Wally an' the rest of the southern gang with him to Red Springs.'

'What!' Nick and Ed gasped together, staring incredulously at Mart.

'The fool!' snarled Ed.

Nick turned to Ed. 'What do we do now?' he asked.

Ed shrugged his shoulders. 'Operate without the southern gang, I reckon, there's not much else we can do.' His eyes narrowed. 'But when I see brother Lee he'll learn who's boss round here,' he hissed venomously from tight lips.

Chapter Two

The sun was nearing noon when a lone, travel-stained cowboy rode into the small town of Apache which nestled under the east side of the Wichita Mountains. The horse, its hoofs hardly stirring the dust, plodded slowly down the main street. The young man examined the buildings as he rode past the houses, the store and the sheriff's office. His impassive face brightened a little when he saw the saloon and two blocks beyond it the town's only hotel.

Joe Burgess guided the animal to the hotel, in front of which he swung from the saddle and stretched himself, easing his limbs after his long ride. Entering the building he booked himself a room and ordered a hot bath before taking his horse to the livery stable.

An hour later, Joe, refreshed by his bath and hot meal, strolled along the sidewalk to the saloon where he found a number of cowboys at the bar and three card games in progress. He ordered a beer and strolled over to the card tables. He studied the play intently and when one of the players pushed his chair back and quit the game, Joe took his place.

He eyed the dealer impassively as he sat down. A tall, thin man with hollow cheeks and pale complexion shuffled the cards deftly with his long, thin fingers. Joe watched the cards knowing that he was being studied by the man opposite to him. The dealer saw a young cowboy, broad-shouldered but of medium build with light-brown hair and sharp-brown eyes. He smiled to himself as he figured that the newcomer was probably fresh from some job and flush with a well-filled pay-roll which, under the guidance of the cards, would change places to his side of the table.

The fortunes of the game flowed back and forth but gradually Joe's usual luck with cards began to leave him and the man opposite smiled as the money came his way.

'Another hand?' he asked, as he gathered the cards and began to shuffle them.

Joe nodded unsmilingly and with half-closed eyes watched the man carefully.

As the last card was dealt, Joe suddenly slammed his hand on to the table startling the other three with the force of the blow.

'You low down, sneaking card-sharp!' yelled Joe.

The gambler stiffened, his eyes narrowed staring coldly at Joe. 'What am I supposed to hev done?' he asked testily.

'Jest dealt yourself an unbeatable hand off the bottom,' snapped Joe.

The dealer grinned. He looked at the other two card players. 'Did you gentlemen see me?' As they shook their heads the gambler turned to Joe. A sneer curled the corners of his mouth. 'There you are,' he said, trying to hold Joe's attention as he moved his hand slowly towards his cards.

Joe suddenly leaned forward, grabbed the cards, and turned them face upwards to reveal an unbeatable hand. The gambler's face hardened, his hand flew to his pocket, but before he could draw the gun Joe's hand closed on his Colt, swivelled it swiftly in its special holster and squeezed the trigger.

The crash of the gun filled the saloon. The man opposite Joe gasped, his eyes widened unbelievingly as he grasped at his stomach and swayed momentarily before pitching forward on to the table.

Joe leaped to his feet dragging his Colt from its holster.

'Don't anyone move,' he snapped, eyeing

20

the occupants of the saloon carefully. He backed slowly towards the batwings until he touched them. He paused to glance round the saloon and then stepped swiftly on to the sidewalk. Ramming his Colt into its holster he spun on his heel and leaped forward to unhitch the nearest horse from the rail.

Feet pounded on the sidewalk and, as Joe leaped into the saddle, he saw two men with stars pinned to their shirts running towards him. He jerked the horse round, kicked it into a gallop, and, as the animal stretched itself, he flattened himself in the saddle.

Seeing the stranger leaping on to the horse the lawmen drew their Colts and fired after the fleeing figure, but Joe Burgess handled the animal skillfully, weaving along the street and the whining bullets whistled harmlessly past.

Sheriff Bill Dawson cursed when he saw the man was escaping. 'Get the horses!' he yelled to his deputy, and hurried forward to the saloon out of which poured most of its occupants. 'What's happened?' shouted Dawson as he ran up.

'Thet hombre shot Connors; accused him of cheatin',' answered one of the men.

The sheriff nodded grimly and stepped off

the sidewalk as his deputy pounded towards him with the horses. As the lawman pulled them to a sliding halt, Dawson grabbed the reins, leaped into the saddle and the two men kicked them into an earth-shaking gallop in pursuit of the killer.

Ed and Nick Brown, accompanied by Mart Webster, pulled their horses to a halt on the side of a hill overlooking the trail which ran south from Apache. They sat easily in the saddle surveying the land below them.

Suddenly Ed stiffened as he stared in the direction of the town.

'Some hombre in a hurry,' he observed, indicating the dust cloud which rose above the trail from Apache.

His companions shaded their eyes against the glare of the sun.

'Yeah,' agreed Nick. 'An' there's someone behind in the same kind of hurry,' he added when he made out a second dust cloud billowing and mingling with that created by the first rider.

'One of those hombres sure sits his horse like Sheriff Dawson,' said Ed quietly.

'Then this cowpoke in front needs some help,' grinned Nick.

'Right,' said Ed. 'Thet hombre's stickin' to

the trail. We'll ride over the spur of this hill, drop down the other side on to the trail an' ride in alongside him, ease him off the trail at Twisting Bends an' lose Dawson in the hills.'

Nick grinned. 'Sheriff's goin' to be mighty sore, an' what a surprise when one man becomes four!'

The three men laughed, pulled their horses round, and sent them along the hillside. Once across the spur they put the animals down the slope to the trail where they halted behind a group of rocks and awaited the rider who pounded towards them.

As he thundered past, Ed Brown stabbed his horse into a fast gallop and, almost at the same moment, Nick and Mart did likewise.

Startled by the sudden pounding behind him, Joe Burgess glanced over his shoulder. Shaken by the sight of three men on his heels, he reached for his Colt.

'Friends!' yelled Ed, who was almost alongside Joe. 'Helpin' you.'

His tone was convincing, and Joe grinned in acknowledgement as the four men thundered towards Twisting Bends.

Ed moved slightly into the lead and when he reached a point where the trail twisted through the broken hillside for half a mile, he turned his horse sharply off the trail into a narrow ravine and pulled it to a halt. As the others milled around him he indicated to them to keep quiet. They steadied their mounts as the pound of hoofs thundered nearer along the trail. The outlaws tensed themselves, their hands resting on the butts of their Colts, but as the lawmen sped past the end of the ravine they relaxed and grinned at each other.

'Thought you'd pulled thet one,' laughed Nick.

Joe Burgess glanced round his rescuers. 'Thanks,' he said, 'I'm mighty grateful for your help.'

'Forgit it,' Ed grinned. 'We don't like the law.' He pulled his horse round. 'C'm on,' he called. 'Let's git some ground between us an' the sheriff before he realises we've given him the slip.' He kicked his horse forward and led the way along a narrow path which twisted up the steep side of the hill.

Sheriff Dawson was startled when he rounded the curve of the hill and saw three riders ranged around the man he was pursuing.

'Where did they come from?' he yelled to his deputy, who shook his head in reply. Although they realised they were outnumbered, neither man eased his pace as their horses flashed across the ground. The lawmen handled their mounts skillfully over the rougher ground as the trail twisted through the broken hillside for half a mile. As they thundered round the last bend the sheriff hauled hard on the reins, bringing his horse to a sliding, dust-stirring halt. His deputy added to the cloud of dust as he pulled on the reins to bring his mount slithering to a stop alongside the sheriff.

'Lost him!' shouted Dawson, as he stared across the countryside ahead. 'Must hev slipped off the trail somewhere through Twisting Bends.'

The two men pulled their horses round and rode at a canter towards the rougher country.

'Careful,' warned the sheriff as they neared the first bend. 'They've plenty of cover to bushwack us.'

The lawmen rode cautiously, searching the hillside as they negotiated the trail, but they rode the half mile without seeing a sign of the men they were pursuing.

'Looks as if they've given us the slip,' said the sheriff. 'They could be headin' anywhere into these mountains.'

The two men searched for half an hour trying to pick up some trail left by the outlaws, but without success.

'Guess we may as well head fer town,' said Dawson wearily.

His deputy nodded, and the lawmen sent their horses at a steady trot towards Apache.

'I guess Sheriff Dawson's hoppin' mad by now,' grinned Ed as the four men rode into camp and slipped from the saddles.

'Thanks again,' said Joe, extending his hand to Ed. 'Name's Joe Burgess.'

Ed took the firm grip. 'Glad to know you,' he said. 'I'm Ed Brown; this is brother Nick, an' this is Mart Webster.'

A look of surprise crossed Joe's face. He nodded to the other two men and looked hard at Ed. 'Ed Brown, leader of the Brown gang?' he asked incredulously.

'Yeah,' answered Ed. 'Glad you've heard of me.'

'Who hasn't in these parts?' replied Joe. 'But you risked…'

'Nothin',' cut in Ed with a laugh. 'I jes' hate to see anyone in trouble with the law. Kansan aren't you?'

Joe nodded. 'Yeah, I've been down in Texas; been ridin' home over the past two years; odd

26

job here, odd job there; you know how it goes.'

Nick, who had been watching Joe shrewdly, stepped forward. 'Why was Sheriff Dawson after you?' he asked curiously.

Joe quickly told his story and, as he finished, Nick glanced at his brother and nodded his head. Ed smiled, knowing that Joe met with Nick's approval.

'Wal, now you're on the run,' said Ed. 'I guess you may as well throw in your lot with us. I need a few more men.'

'Thet suits me fine,' grinned Joe.

'Good, then let's hev some grub,' answered Ed.

Mart Webster was already preparing a meal and soon the four men were enjoying it.

'Which part of Texas hev you come from?' asked Nick.

'Red Springs,' answered Joe. 'But thet was two years ago.'

The mention of Red Springs made Ed look up sharply. His brows puckered as he glanced at Nick who had been equally surprised by Joe's statement.

'What were you doin' down there?' asked Ed, eyeing the cowboy carefully.

'I rode for a Kansas outfit run by two

27

brothers name of Pickering,' replied Joe. 'They got mixed up with a hombre name of Wayman, who owned a big spread near Red Springs. Wayman was killed an' the Pickerings forged a bill of sale showin' Wayman had sold his spread to them. The Texan hed made a will leavin' his property to a brother back east. This brother didn't want it an' had ordered it to be auctioned. The Pickerings arrived jest in time to stop the sale.' Joe took a long drink at his coffee.

'Are they still down there?' asked Nick.

Joe shook his head. 'No,' he replied. 'They started to run foul of the sheriff when they tried to charge a toll fer crossing the Brazo at Wayman's Ford, close to their ranch. One thing led to another but the sheriff was too smart fer them; reckon he'd been suspicious of thet bill of sale all along. Ranch now belongs to the sheriff's father-in-law an' I've heard he gave a sizeable piece to the lawman.'

'Who is this tin star?' asked Ed.

'Hombre name of Dan McCoy,' said Joe.

Ed glanced quickly at Nick. He looked hard at Joe. 'Ever heard of Wes Brown?' he asked suddenly.

Joe rubbed his chin thoughtfully. 'Wes Brown?' he whispered half to himself. 'Never

met anyone by thet name but something...'
He paused, then suddenly his eyes widened.
'Shore, shore, I've heard his name down in
Red Springs. Seems this here Dan McCoy
cleared up some trouble before my time
down there, mingled it rough with this Wes
Brown an' gunned him down in front of the
townsfolk – beat him to the draw.'

Both Ed and Nick looked startled at this
statement.

'Beat him to the draw!' gasped Ed. 'But
Wes was as fast as anyone I've seen except
for Lee.'

'Maybe,' said Joe, 'but McCoy's like light-
ning.' He looked curiously at Ed. 'You knew
this Wes Brown?'

Ed nodded. 'Our brother,' he explained.
'We only heard of his death yesterday an'
brother Lee rode off last night takin' some
of the gang with him, intendin' to blow the
town an' Sheriff McCoy apart.'

'He'll hev to be mighty quick on the draw
to put it over McCoy,' said Joe.

'He went without our approval,' said Nick.
'We've a nice set-up in these hills an' didn't
want it spoiling.'

Ed, who had been staring at the fire
thoughtfully, looked up at Joe. 'We said we'd
get even with McCoy some time. Joe, pitch

in with us, if Lee is successful all well an' good, if not, wal, after what you've told me I've the makings of a scheme in my mind which, with your help, could make that tin star squirm fer a bit before we finish him off.'

Joe pursed his lips thoughtfully before speaking. 'It'll hev to be good to outsmart McCoy, but I'm willin'.'

Chapter Three

Three days after leaving the Wichita Mountains, Lee Brown halted his gang five miles north of Red Springs. 'Reckon this is as good a place as any to camp,' he said, swinging from the saddle. As soon as they had established their camp and had a meal, Lee outlined his plan.

'The sole purpose of this ride is to get the sheriff, if he is still around,' he said, his voice low but filled with determination. 'I aim to gun him down in front of the townsfolk so they'll remember thet no lawman can kill a Brown an' git away with it. We'll ride into town separately tomorrow; I'll see if I can git a line on the sheriff, the rest of you study the lay-out of the place an' meet back here late afternoon.'

The sun was nearing noon when Lee Brown strolled into the sheriff's office in Red Springs.

'Mornin',' he greeted.

The grizzled-faced, weather-beaten, grey-haired man behind the desk looked up.

31

'Howdy, stranger,' he said. 'What can I do fer you?'

'I've jest been told in the saloon thet Sheriff McCoy's out of town,' replied Lee, 'any idea when he'll be back?'

Clint looked shrewdly at the man in front of him. 'I can handle anythin' whilst the sheriff is away,' he replied icily.

Lee grinned. 'Not this,' he said. 'It's a personal message for McCoy.'

Clint straightened himself in his chair. 'I'm Dan's deputy; I served as his father's deputy before him; there ain't any of their personal affairs they wouldn't trust me with,' he answered curtly.

Lee shoved his sombrero to the back of his head. He smiled amiably and shrugged his shoulders. 'You'll be Clint Schofield; I've heard a lot about you, but nevertheless I was told to deliver this message to no one but McCoy. I'm sorry, it's not thet I don't trust you; it's jest that I obey orders especially when I get paid for carryin' them out.'

The deputy's face softened. 'I'm sorry fer speakin' sharply,' he apologised. 'This is the first time I've had this happen an'...'

'No offence meant,' cut in Lee pleasantly. 'But can you tell me when he'll be back?'

'Difficult to say,' replied Clint. 'He's away

32

seein' his brother an' didn't know definitely when he would be back.'

'I'll be ridin' this way in a week or two,' drawled Lee, turning towards the door. 'Reckon I'll look him up then.'

Who should I say wants to see him?' asked Clint.

'He won't know me, but my name's Lee Westland,' lied the outlaw, thinking it wisest not to reveal his real name. He swung out of the door and as it shut Clint stared at it thoughtfully.

Lee Brown strolled slowly along the sidewalk. He felt that the deputy had not told him all he knew about McCoy's absence. He stopped when he reached two cowboys who were leaning against the rail along the edge of the boards.

'Mornin',' greeted Lee pleasantly. 'Could you direct me to Dan McCoy's house?'

'Shore,' answered the taller of the two men, straightening up. 'Take the second turning on the left. About a hundred yards an' you'll see a house set back, thet's it. Sheriff's out of town, but you'll find his wife at home.'

'Thanks,' replied Lee and strolled casually in the direction indicated.

When he turned the corner the outlaw saw

a small, neat, freshly painted house standing back about thirty yards from the dusty road. The garden was neat and well cared-for and the whole property was surrounded by a strong white fence. Lee pushed open the gate and followed the path to the four steps which led on to a veranda which ran the full-length of the front of the house.

Lee rapped on the door, and a few moments later it was opened by a smartly dressed young woman.

'Mornin' ma'am,' greeted Lee, touching his hat. 'I'm tryin' to get in touch with Dan McCoy.'

'I'm sorry he's out of town, but I'm his wife; can I help you?' she answered.

Lee was surprised; he had expected to find someone much older, but now he could not help admiring the pretty, dark-haired young woman, whose dark-brown eyes smiled a greeting.

'Wal, I don't think so, Mrs McCoy,' replied Lee. 'It was a personal matter. Any idea when he'll be back?'

'It's difficult to say,' said Barbara McCoy. 'He's been to Santa Rosa to see his brother, but I do know he's on his way home. I reckon he should be here within the next three days.'

'I see,' said Lee thoughtfully. 'I don't think it's any good hangin' around here. I'm likely to be back this way in a week or two; I can look him up then.'

'Very good,' said Barbara. 'Can I give him a message or tell him who called?'

'No, it's all right,' answered Lee. 'My name won't mean a thing to him. Goodbye Ma'am.' Lee touched his hat, turned and walked back to the main street.

After having a beer in the Silver Dollar, he rode slowly northwards out of town, and made his way back to camp. The sun was lowering in the west as the five members of the Brown gang rode into camp. They reported their observations to Lee who, during the evening meal, had little to say. It was not until the meal was over and his men had settled themselves around the fire with their cheroots and cigarettes that Lee unfolded his plans.

'McCoy is on his way back from New Mexico,' he explained, 'so he'll approach Red Springs along the west road. Jake an' Bud take up a spot about ten miles along thet road an' watch out fer McCoy.'

'I got an idea what this McCoy looks like,' said Wally. 'Thought it might be useful to know.'

'Good work,' praised Lee eagerly.

'He's about twenty-seven, tall, slim, good looking in a rugged, weather-beaten way, blue eyes, fair hair,' explained Wally.

Jake and Bud listened intently. 'What do you want us to do when we spot him?' asked Jake.

'The rest of us will stay here until we hear from you,' replied Lee. 'As soon as you see McCoy, Jake, you will ride back here. Bud, you tail McCoy to town. When you reach Red Springs you will stay at the west end to block any escape thet way. Red, you'll do the same at the east end. Jake an' Slim will clear the street, an' Wally will accompany me to Mrs McCoy's after which I will be in the main street to call out McCoy in front of the townsfolk.' Lee went on to instruct his men more carefully in their individual tasks.

After breakfast the following morning, Jake and Bud saddled their horses and were soon taking the west road out of Red Springs. They had ridden about eleven miles when Jake indicated a small, rocky hill a short distance ahead.

'Reckon thet will probably suit us,' he said. 'The rocks should give cover an' we should have a good view of the trail from up there.'

The two men kicked their horses into a

gallop, and were soon dismounting at the bottom of the hillock. They scrambled quickly amongst the rocks, and when they reached the top, wide grins split their faces.

'Ideal,' said Bud enthusiastically.

The hillock was situated close to the edge of a gentle slope, down which the trail wound gradually until it reached the floor of a wide valley.

'We'll pick him out miles off,' grinned Jake eagerly. 'I'll git a good start before he reaches here. Let's make ourselves comfortable; we may be here for a few days.'

The two men returned to their horses and after securing them they returned to the top of the hillock and made camp.

The sun was blazing from a cloudless sky, and Jake wiped the sweat from his face as he leaned back against a rock, wishing he could find some shade. Jake was restless; he hated this waiting and watching which had now moved into its third day. He leaned his head against the rock and tipped his sombrero forward over his eyes.

'Jake! Jake!'

The man was startled from his dozing by the urgency of the call. He pushed the sombrero from his eyes and twisted round to see Bud shouting to him from the rocks above.

'Hombre riding this way,' shouted Bud when he saw Jake stir.

The outlaw pushed himself to his feet and scrambling up the hillside, was soon stretched beside Bud, looking over the wide valley. He narrowed his eyes against the glare and made out the figure of a lone rider through the shimmering haze. He took the spyglass offered by Bud and drew the rider into focus.

'Could be,' he muttered, and waited for the man to come nearer.

Bud tapped the ground impatiently as the rider kept to a walking place, conserving his energy and that of his horse in the heat of the day.

Jake raised the spy-glass again. Suddenly he stiffened, peering more intently at the approaching figure.

Eagerly he passed the spy-glass to Bud. 'Reckon it's him,' he said excitedly.

Bud stared at the rider for a few moments. 'Guess so,' he agreed. 'You'd better git word to Lee. You'll hev plenty of time the way this hombre's ridin'.'

Jake slithered quickly down the hillside, and was soon heading for the outlaw camp.

'He's comin', boss,' yelled Jake as he pulled his horse to a sliding halt.

'How far off?' asked Lee eagerly.

'You've plenty of time,' explained Jake. 'He's riding slow in this heat.'

'Good,' replied Lee. 'Saddle up, boys,' he ordered.

The outlaws broke camp quickly and were soon riding towards Red Springs. They halted at the end of the main street and Lee was pleased to see that the mid-day heat had driven most people indoors. Only two cowboys lazed in chairs outside the Wells Fargo office, and two others strolled casually along the sidewalk on the other side of the street.

'Red, you stay at this end of town,' ordered Lee. 'Jake, Slim, leave your horses here. Slim, you take the right-hand side of the street an' clear everyone thet's about into the store. Jake, do the same on the left, an' git anyone about into the saloon. Then post yourselves at the doors ready fer McCoy if things should go wrong.' Lee turned to Wally. 'We'll pay a visit to Mrs McCoy,' he said, an evil grin splitting his face.

The two men rode along the main street and turned off to dismount in front of McCoy's house. They hurried up the path and Lee knocked sharply at the door which was opened a few moments later by Mrs McCoy.

'Afternoon, ma'am,' greeted Lee pleasantly.

'Oh, it's you again,' answered Barbara. 'I'm sorry but my husband hasn't returned yet.'

'I know,' replied Lee, 'but he's headin' this way now, may we come in and wait?'

Barbara stared at the two men, surprise showing in her eyes.

'But...' she began, only to be cut short when Lee pushed her roughly into the house. He stepped quickly inside followed by Wally, who closed the door behind them.

'Mrs McCoy,' said Lee curtly. 'I hev a message fer your husband here,' he added, tapping his holster, 'an' I want no interference from you.'

Barbara stared wide-eyed at the two men. Fear for her husband crossed her face as the full realisation of Lee's meaning bit into her mind.

'What's he done to you?' she gasped.

'Not to me,' replied Lee. 'But he gunned down my brother. Remember Wes Brown?'

'Wes Brown!' Barbara's voice was hardly above a whisper.

40

Lee nodded. 'Get some things together, quick. Wally's takin' you out of town.' He turned to Wally. 'Take her to Ed an' Nick; if anythin' happens to me they may find her useful when they get around to dealin' with McCoy. Get her out of here quick; she mustn't be around when her husband rides in.'

Barbara looked round desperately seeking some means of escape, but she realised it was useless. Wally stepped forward and pushed her roughly towards the stairs.

'Two minutes to git your things,' he snapped. 'Or I take you as you are.'

Lee moved to the door and grinned when he saw Wally take the precaution of following Barbara upstairs. He knew Barbara would not give Wally the slip.

When Slim and Jake saw Lee and Wally turn off the main street they moved quickly along the sidewalk. Slim stopped outside the Wells Fargo office and seeing no one inside guessed that the two men in the chairs were the officials.

One of them glanced up at Slim. 'Want somethin'?' he drawled lazily.

Slim drew his Colt. 'Yeah,' he replied. 'Git on your feet.'

41

The two men stared incredulously at him, but seeing the threatening look on his face they pushed themselves slowly to their feet.

'You're wastin' your time,' spluttered one of the men. 'There's very little cash in the office.'

'I don't want your cash,' snapped Slim. 'Now shut up an' git to the store.'

The two men shuffled along the sidewalk, urged on by Slim. When they reached the store the outlaw ordered them inside where he found the storekeeper serving two cowboys. All three stared in amazement when they saw the two Wells Fargo men enter the store at the point of a gun.

Slim stood beside the door. He saw that none of the men wore holsters. 'All of you over there,' he snapped indicating a place against the window, where he could keep his eye on them from outside. 'Don't try anythin', especially when McCoy rides in,' he warned. 'I can still see you from outside.'

Jake walked quickly to the sheriff's office where Clint gasped when he looked up from some papers he was examining to find himself staring into the cold muzzle of a Colt.

'On your feet, old timer,' snapped Jake. Clint pushed himself from his chair, eyeing the stranger shrewdly. 'Unbuckle your gun belt,' ordered the outlaw.

Clint weighed his chances as his hands moved slowly towards his belt, but he realised it was hopeless with a Colt pointing straight at his heart. He unbuckled his belt, which fell to the floor with a dull thud.

A smile flickered across Jake's mouth. He motioned towards the door with his gun. 'Outside,' he ordered. 'To the saloon.'

Wondering what this was all about, Clint did as he was told and, as they entered the saloon, he felt the Colt pressed hard into his back and the whispered 'Hold it' brought him to a halt.

'Quiet; everyone!' yelled Jake as he stepped back and to one side of the deputy sheriff. A gasp of astonishment filled the room when the ten cowboys saw the Colt pointing at Clint.

'Take it easy,' shouted Jake. 'One false move an' this hombre gets some lead. Jest ease your guns out of their holsters gentle like, an' throw them outside.' His eyes narrowed, ready for any suspicious move, as he watched the occupants of the saloon do as they were ordered.

When the last gun had been thrown outside, Jake shoved Clint forward towards the bar. The old man stumbled and would have fallen but for two cowboys who caught him. A tall man stepped forward menacingly, only to halt as Jake swung his gun on him.

'I wouldn't if I were you,' he hissed. 'An' don't anyone make a false move or sound, especially when your no good sheriff rides in.'

Clint was startled by these last words. 'Dan isn't around,' he said hesitantly.

Jake grinned, showing yellow teeth. 'You'll see,' he replied with a chuckle. 'An' Lee Brown has a surprise waiting for him.'

Clint stiffened. 'Lee Brown!' he whispered, half to himself. His thoughts raced; the man who had introduced himself a few days ago as Lee Westland had had a familiar look about him; now Clint knew; he bore some resemblance to Wes Brown. 'A revenge killin'!' muttered Clint. His brain pounded, desperately trying to think of some way of warning Dan, but he realized that even if it was possible to outsmart this cowpoke, there must be others about.

'All of you git over by the bar so's I can keep my eyes on you from the window whilst I'm outside,' ordered Jake, as he backed towards the door. He stepped outside quickly, moved swiftly along the sidewalk, and took

44

up a position near the window. A sharp blow with the muzzle of his colt shattered the glass. He poked the gun through menacingly. 'Jest stay where you are, nice an' easy like,' he called out, his voice full of meaning for anyone who stepped out of line.

When Lee Brown rode slowly back into the main street he grunted with satisfaction at seeing Slim and Jake leaning against the walls of the store and the saloon. With a brief nod to them he rode along the street, dismounting a short distance beyond the saloon. He tied his horse to the rail, stepped on to the sidewalk and, after easing his Colt in its holster, he leaned on the rail watching the west road into town.

Chapter Four

Dan McCoy eased himself in the saddle as he topped the long slope out of the valley and put his horse into a steady trot towards Red Springs.

It was good to be back on familiar ground after his absence in Santa Rosa. The delay in Roaring Valley on his way back had been irksome, and now he looked forward eagerly to seeing Barbara and holding her in his arms again.

As he increased his pace a lone cowboy, who watched him from the cover of some rocks, slipped unobtrusively on to the trail and shadowed him to Red Springs.

Before reaching the main street Dan turned on to a back trail which brought him to his house before meeting any of the town's people. Bud halted and watched him for a while before riding to the end of the main street where he took up his appointed position after signalling his arrival to Lee Brown.

Dan slipped from the saddle and hurried

up the path, surprised that Barbara had not seen him.

'Babs,' he called, as he stepped inside the house, but only the house echoed his shout. He pushed open the door of the kitchen where he saw the table was set for a meal which had not been started. He hurried through all the rooms, but there was no sign of his wife. 'Can't be far with thet meal all ready,' he muttered to himself as he came down the stairs. 'Guess Babs won't be long.'

He went outside, and after stabling his horse, he returned to the house and washed off the dust of the trail. Half an hour passed, and Dan, growing a little uneasy, picked up his sombrero and hurried along the road, pausing when he reached Main Street.

He glanced up and down the street and was surprised to see only three men on the sidewalks. They were strangers to him; not one familiar face was in sight. He was struck by the fact that the three men were positioned separately and as he looked round, he saw a man at each end of the town. No one stirred. A frightening silence hung over Main Street. Tension filled the air. Dan was puzzled.

'Five,' he muttered to himself. 'But why?'

The men appeared not to notice him, but,

as he stepped forward and crossed the road towards the sheriff's office, he felt their eyes on him, watching every step and every movement that he made.

He pushed open the door of the office and found what he half expected to find as he crossed the street; the office was empty. Something was wrong, but what, and why? Dan closed the door quietly and turned round slowly. The saloon was the place for information, but as Dan moved forward he saw the man who leaned on the rail straighten and step down on to the dusty road.

'McCoy? Are you Sheriff McCoy?' yelled the stranger.

Dan halted in his tracks. He saw the men on either side of the street straighten and their hands moved nearer their holsters. The sheriff hesitated for a moment, and then stepped off the sidewalk so that he had the three men well in view.

'I'm McCoy,' shouted Dan. 'What do you want?'

'You,' replied the stranger, and moved slowly along the street offering no more information until he halted about twelve yards in front of Dan. 'I go by the name of Lee Brown,' he called.

'Brown!' Dan's thoughts raced. 'It couldn't be, not all this time after; and yet...'

A cold, icy grin crossed Brown's face. 'Yeah. I'm Wes Brown's brother; surprised Mister Sheriff?'

Dan did not answer. Suddenly he realised this man was here with one purpose and there was no avoiding the gun fight!

'Don't look fer help, McCoy,' continued Brown. 'We've got thet angle tied up.' He saw the sheriff glance at the Colts scattered outside the saloon. 'There ain't anyone in there can help you.'

Dan eyed Brown carefully. He knew he was out on his own with three men ready to gun him down, and yet he felt the position was not hopeless. He guessed Brown would play a lone hand first to satisfy his ego. A calmness flooded through his body as he relaxed, his hand hanging limp, close to his Colt.

'Barbara!' Horror suddenly filled Dan's mind. Was Brown at the bottom of her absence?

'What hev you done with my wife?' Dan hissed venomously.

Lee laughed. 'You catch on fast, McCoy,' he called. 'She's taken a little ride. Reckon my brothers might find her useful if anything

49

goes wrong here. But thet isn't likely, is it?' Hate filled his eyes as he stared at Dan. 'We've talked enough, McCoy,' he rapped viciously.

The words had hardly passed his lips when his hand flashed to his Colt. The gun leaped from the holster, but the pressure was barely on the trigger when Dan fired. Brown's knees started to buckle, a look of amazement on his face at the speed of the draw. As he fell his finger tightened on the trigger and Dan felt the lead crash into his left arm as he dived forward firing at the man in front of the saloon.

So swift had Dan reacted that Jake's Colt never left its holster. As he hit the ground Dan twisted. A bullet hit the dust close to his face, and another clipped his Stetson as it fell from his head. Dan squeezed his trigger again and again and saw the man near the store stagger backwards against the wall. Slim jerked his gun upwards, but the bullet whined over Dan as he rolled over nearer the sidewalk to send a third bullet into the outlaw who slid slowly down the wall to lie still in a crumpled heap.

The batwings of the Silver Dollar burst open, and Clint leaped forward to grab a gun from the ground. He spotted Red at the east end of the street and loosed off two shots in his direction to hasten his leap for his horse.

At the west end of the town, Bud had been so amazed at the swiftness of the execution of his fellow outlaws that he stood frozen to the spot, but as Clint swung round he dived to his horse behind the nearest building and in a second was galloping away from Red Springs as if the devil was chasing him.

Men poured from the saloon and the store, but Clint was the first to reach Dan as he climbed to his feet.

'You all right?' asked the deputy anxiously.

'Sure,' replied Dan. 'It's just a flesh wound.' His face was grim. 'Brown said he'd kidnapped Babs, sent her to his brothers.'

'What!' gasped Clint.

'Didn't know Wes Brown hed any brothers,' went on Dan.

'I've been doin' some thinkin', since I knew that was Lee Brown,' said Clint. 'It all came back to me, there are two other brothers, Ed an' Nick. I've never seen them, but I recall Wes talking about them.'

'I've got to find them. Babs is in danger,' said Dan urgently.

'Ever heard of the Brown gang which rode through Missouri, Kansas an' Colorado an'

51

is now operatin' in Oklahoma?'

Dan nodded. 'Sure but...'

'I figure thet's where we'll hev to look,' cut in Clint.

'You could be right,' replied Dan excitedly. 'But not "we", someone has to stop here and keep law in Red Springs. I'll go right away.'

'You can't tackle a gang alone,' answered Clint. 'If I can't go take Jack and Howard Collins with you?'

'Good idea,' agreed Dan. 'Let's git out to the Bar X.'

The two men soon had their horses ready and it was not long before they were riding up to the Bar X ranch-house standing close to Wayman's Ford on the Brazo River. Bill Collins and his two sons hurried to greet them.

'Howdy, Dan. Glad to see you back,' welcomed his father-in-law, gripping his hand warmly.

'What happened to you?' asked Jack, indicating Dan's arms as he and Howard gave him a welcoming slap on the back.

'It's good to see you all. Got this in town,' Dan said, and went to explain what had happened. 'I'm heading for Oklahoma straight away,' he concluded.

Jack and Howard glanced at their father who knew their unspoken thoughts.

'The boys will ride with you, Dan,' said Bill Collins without hesitation. 'This is not the homecoming Barbara planned for you,' he went on as Jack and Howard hurried to get their horses ready.

Dan looked curiously at his father-in-law, who went on to explain. 'I always said my property would be divided three ways between Babs, Jack an' Howard, wal Babs knew you were keen to start ranching, so I agreed to let her have her share now. I signed the Circle C over to her, and she's hed it made over to you. She's been doin' a lot of preparations over there.'

Dan gasped at this news. 'Gee, Mr Collins this is mighty generous of you,' he said excitedly. 'I always figured I'd get a small spread when I retired, but this ... wal ... I reckon with a competent foreman, I can run the ranch and still be sheriff.' The look on his face became grim. 'But it's no use without Barbara, I've got to find her first.'

53

Chapter Five

Wally kept to a hard pace throughout the afternoon and when he pulled to a halt in the shelter of some bushes close to the Wichita River, Barbara was too weary to attempt to escape. They had just settled down for the night when the sound of hoofs broke the silence. Barbara sat up, an eager look at the anticipation of rescue in her eyes. Wally grabbed his gun.

'Not a sound,' he hissed menacingly.

He jumped to his feet and kicked out the low embers of the fire hoping that its light had not been seen by the riders.

A few moments later when he heard the horses turn off the trail he knew he had been too late. He stepped swiftly backwards until he was behind Barbara, his gun held ready.

'Hold it!' he called, clicking back the hammer of the Colt ominously.

Two men froze in their tracks.

'Thet you, Wally?' called one.

'Yeah,' replied the outlaw. 'Who's thet?'

'Red an' Bud,' came the answer.

Wally relaxed, slipped the Colt back into the leather and stepped forward to greet the two men. Barbara sank back on the ground, tears of disappointment welling in her eyes.

'Where's Lee?' asked Wally anxiously, as Bud and Red joined him.

'The sheriff got him,' answered Red. 'I've never seen anythin' so fast. He got Jake an' Slim as well.'

'What!' Wally stared incredulously at the two outlaws.

Bud went on to relate the story of the shooting and Barbara, brushing away her tears, felt greatly relieved to know that Dan was all right. She felt sure that he would soon be following their trail, but suddenly she realised that he would have no idea what had happened to her. Tears flowed freely and she sobbed herself to sleep.

'I guess Lee's precautions are goin' to pay off,' laughed Red, indicating Barbara.

The outlaws rode hard all the next day and it was late evening when the light of a camp fire in a small hollow indicated the end of their journey.

'Who's there?'

A cry from the darkness caused Wally to pull his horse to a standstill.

55

'Wally,' he answered quickly.

'Come forward,' came the reply.

The outlaw led his party into the light of the camp fire where the riders slipped wearily from the saddles.

'Who's this?' asked Ed, surprised to see a female amongst the riders.

'Mrs Dan McCoy,' explained Wally.

'What the...' burst out Nick. 'Where's Lee?'

Mart Webster took charge of the horses, and Wally told the story of their expedition to Red Springs.

Hate smouldered in Ed's eyes when he learned of Lee's death. His lips tightened as he eyed Barbara.

'I'll shore make that tin-star wish he'd never heard the name of Brown before I'm through,' he hissed venomously.

'Does this alter our plans?' asked Nick.

Ed paced in front of the fire and Barbara recoiled from the evil look of hate on the outlaw's face.

'I said I was all fer making McCoy squirm,' replied Ed. 'Wal, I figure we should make him squirm twice as much now. We'll do it the way we planned after we've cleared up the few jobs we've arranged up here. We've got Mrs McCoy; Lee was mighty wise to send us a hostage; an' I figure thet two bit sheriff will play right into our hands when he finds out thet we hev her.'

About the same time as Wally led his party into the camp, three dust-stained, travel-weary cowboys were riding into the small town of Apache in the shadow of the Wichita Mountains. Dan had pressed the ride hard, anxious to be into the area in which the Browns were last known to have operated.

They dismounted in front of the hotel and, noting the livery stable a short distance down the street, Jack Collins took charge of the horses whilst Dan and Howard booked the rooms.

After a wash and a meal Dan went in search of the sheriff. He saw a light shining from the lawman's office and Dan stepped inside.

'Evenin' sheriff,' greeted Dan. 'I'd like some information from you.'

The sheriff eyed the stranger curiously. He saw a likeable, upright, well-built, young man whose keen sharp eyes he knew would miss nothing. He noted the long, supple fingers and guessed this cowboy knew how to handle himself and his gun.

57

'I'll do what I can,' replied the sheriff.

'I'd better introduce myself,' went on Dan. 'I'm Dan McCoy, Sheriff of Red Springs down in Texas.' He saw the man behind the desk glance at his shirt. 'No, I'm not wearin' my badge. I don't want it to be known around here thet I'm a Sheriff.'

'Pull up a chair,' said Sheriff Dawson, introducing himself and gripping Dan's extended hand. 'What's the trouble?'

Dan explained his mission. 'So you see,' he concluded, 'the sooner I git on the trail of these Browns the better I'll like it.'

'They run a mighty big outfit in the mountains,' said Dawson. 'We keep gettin' a few of them, but they keep gettin' recruits an' we've never been able to flush out the leaders. They raid everywhere, north, south, east, and west. It's thought there's a gang on each side of the mountains an' thet the Browns control it from some central point.'

'Where did the last raid take place?' asked Dan.

'In the west,' answered the sheriff. 'But the next one could be anywhere. The best place to get near the Browns is in Lone Wolf, on the north side of the Wichitas. Lone Wolf puts on a face, but strictly speaking it's an outlaw town – run by the Browns for their gang. If you go up there watch your step; it's the most lawless part of the State.'

'Wal, I reckon thet's where we'll head fer in the morning,' said Dan, rising to his feet. 'If you git any leads maybe you'll try to contact me.'

'Sure,' agreed Dawson.

'Thanks,' said Dan and bidding the sheriff goodnight he hastened back to the hotel where he quickly told the Collins brothers of his interview with the sheriff.

Three men, their faces and clothes covered with dust, rode slowly along the short main street of Lone Wolf. It had little to recommend it as a town, boast – one saloon, one dilapidated hotel, one store, a livery stable and about ten houses. The saloon was the biggest building and its new coat of paint was in marked contrast to the shabbiness of the other wooden erections.

As they rode, Dan McCoy looked in vain for the sheriff's office. He realised that this was truly what Sheriff Dawson had said, 'a lawless town', and Dan felt that if they were to get near the Browns, it would be here.

The three men pulled their horses to a halt in front of the hotel and when they eventually found the proprietor asleep in a back room, they were shown quickly up the stairs to three rooms which were furnished with only the bare necessities.

As the proprietor turned to leave Dan halted him. 'We were told we could contact the Brown gang here, know any of them?'

The thin, pale-faced proprietor, his shoulders hunched as if he was permanently prepared to suffer a blow across them, looked miserably at Dan. 'You want to be in the saloon,' he muttered. 'All the gang get in there some time or another. It's the only place worth having in this one-eyed place.'

'Not much custom?' asked Dan, knowing the answer before he put the question.

'No,' replied the proprietor. 'Who'd want to come here? Looked like growin' into a thrivin' place when I came, but the Browns stepped in an' thet did it.'

'What did they want here?' asked Dan.

'Jest a lawless town where the gang could come; a place which became known fer its unsavoury reputation therefore attracted no-good cowpokes whom the Browns could use.' The man stopped and spluttered, a frightened look crossing his face as he glanced sharply at the men in front of him. 'No offence to you, you know,' he stuttered apologetically.

Dan laughed loudly. 'Fergit it,' he grinned. 'Think you can rustle up some grub fer us?'

'Reckon so,' replied the proprietor, relief showing in his voice, and he hurried from the room.

After the meal Dan and the Collins brothers hurried along the sidewalk to the saloon, swung through the batwings to find the room crowded with men and a few 'saloon-girls'. A piano could be heard faintly above the noise and as Dan led the way to the bar his eyes quickly noted the lay-out of the saloon. The gleaming counter ran almost the full length of one wall, and the rest of the room was filled with small tables, some of which were being used for gambling. A wide staircase led to a balcony which occupied three sides of the building.

Dan called for three beers and when the bar-tender returned with the drinks Dan delayed him.

'I've heard the Browns operate in these parts, know how I can contact them?'

The bar-tender stared wide-eyed at Dan for a moment without speaking. He had never known anyone ride into Lone Wolf and ask that question before.

'Wal,' drawled Howard, 'lost your tongue?'

The barman looked at the three men

61

curiously, then suddenly spun on his heel and without a word hurried to the far end of the bar where the three Texans saw him speak quietly to a man and nod in their direction.

'Guess thet hombre runs this joint,' murmured Jack, noting the frock coat and fancy waistcoat.

'Wait to see what happens,' whispered Dan leaning forward on the counter and sipping his beer.

When the bar-tender moved away and continued to serve the customers Dan saw the well-dressed sleek-haired man watching them curiously as he lit a cheroot. Five minutes passed before he pushed himself from the bar and strolled slowly in the direction of the three Texans who made no move although they knew the man was approaching them.

'Strangers around here?'

Dan turned slowly, leaned back against the bar with his elbows resting on the counter. The Collins brothers straightened and half turned. For a moment Dan did not speak, but looked the man up and down.

'Thet's right,' he drawled.

'Where you from?' asked the man quietly.

'Texas,' replied Dan.

'What you want up here?'

'Guess you already know,' said Dan nodding in the direction of the bar-tender.

The man grinned. 'You miss nothin',' he said. 'What do you want with the Browns?'

'Reckon we can do them a bit of good if we work with them,' drawled Dan.

A faint smile flickered the man's face. He blew a long cloud of smoke into the air and observed Dan shrewdly. 'Got a high opinion of yourself,' he said. 'Wonder if you can match those words?'

'Shore we can,' grinned Dan.

The man looked hard at them for a moment and then without another word turned and strolled casually away. Dan was thoughtful as he watched him climb the stairs slowly, walk along the balcony, knock on a door, and hesitate before opening it and stepping into a room.

'Now's the time,' whispered Dan.

He pushed himself away from the bar and crossed to a nearby table at which sat three cowboys and three girls. He leaned on the table and the three men eyed him with a mixture of surprise and suspicion, whilst the girls looked at him curiously.

'Wal, what do you want?' drawled a big, dark-stubbled-chinned cowboy.

'I reckon this little lady would suit me fine,' grinned Dan, winking at the red-head sitting next to the man who had spoken.

She smiled at Dan as his hand touched hers. The gesture was not lost upon the cowboy who sprang to his feet, sending his chair crashing to the floor. He leaned across the table, grabbed Dan's shirt with one hand, and drew the other back, but before he could deliver the blow Dan's hands grasped the man's arm and with a sharp jerk, yanked him across the table. As the man slid past, Dan drove his fist into his mouth sending him sprawling on to the floor.

'Don't come thet game with me,' snapped McCoy. He turned and held out his arm to the girl, who took it with a smile.

The other two cowboys were on their feet and as Dan turned towards the counter they reached for their Colts.

'Hold it!' Howard's voice rapped clearly as he and Jack stepped forward with Colts facing the two men. Their hands froze on the butts then slowly dropped to their sides.

There was a snarl from the floor and the dark cowboy lunged to his feet and dived at Dan's legs. The lawman, half expecting the attack, turned and stepping to one side

64

raised his knee, catching the man full in the face. The force dropped him to the floor where he lay gasping for breath. Hatred blazed in his eyes as he pushed himself to his feet.

'I'm not through yet,' he snarled. 'I'll make you eat dirt for this.'

Dan pushed the girl to one side as he faced the cowboy, realising that he had to deal with a man who was as strong as an ox. The man leaped forward suddenly, catching Dan half off his guard. He grasped him round the middle pinning his arms to his sides. His grip tightened, driving the breath from Dan's body. Slowly the pressure increased as Dan tried to free his arms but failed. His brain pounded and McCoy knew that unless he could do something quick this man would not hesitate to crack his ribs. Desperately Dan drew his knee sharply upwards, driving it into the cowboy's stomach. Although he was not able to use his full force, his action took the man by surprise and as the grip momentarily relaxed, Dan jerked one arm free and smashed his fist into the stubbled chin. A roar of anger filled the room as the man seized Dan firmly, lifted him off his feet and flung him on to the floor. Dan crashed against the bar; his head spun as he gulped air into his aching lungs. Through the haze in front of his eyes he saw the cowboy lunge towards him and kick wildly at him. Dan twisted and felt the boot just graze the side of his head and crash into the bottom of the counter. In a flash Dan grasped the man's leg and with a sharp pull threw the man to the floor. Dan scrambled to his knees and dived on to the man, pounding his face with his fist. The cowboy raised his knee to send Dan flying over his head. Both men lunged to their feet and as the dark-faced cowboy leaped at him, Dan side-stepped and drove his fist hard into his face to send him sprawling against the counter. His knees started to buckle and as he began to slide to the floor Dan turned to the girl. Although his senses were reeling the man saw his chance; he grasped the counter with his left hand, steadied himself and with his right hand drew a knife from his belt. He drew his arm back, but before he could throw the knife it was sent spinning from his hand as a shot roared around the saloon.

'Hold it,' snapped a voice.

Dan spun round to see a smoking Colt in the hand of a man on the balcony. He judged him to be about thirty-five and saw

66

he was neatly turned out in work-a-day clothes. He was tall, broad-shouldered and his brown hair was brushed neatly back.

'All right everybody,' the man shouted, 'back to your drinks.' His voice was sharp and clear and carried a note of authority with it. 'You,' he called, indicating Dan, 'come up here an' bring your friends with you.'

Dan nodded at Jack and Howard and, as he turned towards the stairs, he tapped the red-head playfully. 'See you later, honey,' he drawled.

As Dan led the way up the stairs he saw the man slip his Colt back into its holster, turn and walk into a room. The man in the fancy waistcoat, to whom Dan had spoken at the bar, was standing beside the open door and indicated to the three Texans to enter.

The man who had fired the Colt was sitting beside a table in the small, neatly-furnished room. He eyed Dan and the Collins brothers shrewdly as he sipped at his whisky.

'Who are you an' where are you from?' he asked. His voice was harsh but full of authority and Dan reckoned that he was facing a man who was accustomed to being obeyed without question.

67

'Dan Ferguson,' came the lawman's reply, 'an' this is Jack Alvaston an' his brother Howard.' The man at the table nodded but afforded the brothers only a cursory glance. 'We come from Texas,' went on Dan, 'but we've been operatin' way north of here.'

'What do you want in Lone Wolf?'

'I reckon you already know,' answered Dan with a grin, nodding in the direction of the man in the fancy waistcoat, who was standing with his back to the door.

The outlaw's face darkened at this remark and Dan figured that he was used to receiving straight replies to his questions; a man who revelled in the authority he had, limited though it may be to a small group within a bigger set up. Because of this he was all the more dangerous, ready to wield his limited power to try to impress the man above him. Dan tested his theory adding quickly. 'It's the Browns I want to see. I'll talk to them; I only deal with top men.'

The outlaw's eyes blazed angrily. 'You'll deal with me or no one!' he snarled. 'Ask anyone who's boss round here; they'll tell you, Curt Jackson; isn't that so Ward?'

'Shore is,' drawled Ward. 'You'd better git it straight Ferguson, the Browns rely a lot on their top men like Curt here, an' if you don't meet with his approval you'll not meet with theirs.'

'If you understand thet, then we might talk,' snapped Jackson. 'I liked the way you handled yourself downstairs, an' I'm short of a few men but if...'

'Then we're just the men you want,' interrupted Dan with a smile.

'Are you?' drawled Jackson wryly. 'Thet remains to be seen. I want to know more about you first.'

'I told you we come from Texas,' answered Dan. 'When things got to hot fer us down there we went north to Kansas, operated there an' over the border into Colorado. Banks, offices, stages, the usual run of things. Came in fer attention.'

'If things were goin' all right, why come down here?' asked Jackson.

'Heard the Browns operated on a big scale an' we figured there'd be more to pick up in a bigger organisation,' explained Dan.

Jackson grunted. 'Seem to know what you're on, Ferguson. Stick around a few days whilst I think things over. I'll contact...'

'A few days,' interrupted Howard stormily. 'Time's money to us, if you've got nothin' here then we'll move on. Seems this isn't the set-up we heard about.'

A smile crossed Jackson's face slowly as he watched Howard. 'Calm down, Alvaston,' he said. 'We operate as the Browns order an' they know what's big enough to be worthwhile.' He eased himself out of his chair. 'Stick around,' he added. 'You'll be in if the Browns approve.'

Ward opened the door and Dan knew there was nothing more to be said. He turned to Jack and Howard. 'C'm on,' he said. 'I reckon we can spare a day or two.'

The three men strolled from the room and as they walked down the stairs they noticed the three cowboys and the three girls were watching them. Dan grinned as he walked up to the table. The dark, stubbled-chinned man stiffened as Dan approached. His lips tightened, his eyes narrowed, glaring angrily at McCoy but watching ever move closely.

As he reached the table Dan slapped the cowboy on the back. 'No hard feelings,' he laughed. 'You can hev her tonight.' He smiled at the redhead. 'Maybe I'll see you tomorrow, honey.' He turned and strolled from the saloon, followed by Jack and Howard.

'Is it wise to hang around this town?' asked Howard, as they walked along the sidewalk towards the hotel.

'We hev no other choice at the moment,' replied Dan. 'If we're to get near the Browns it will be from here.'

Chapter Six

Two days later when Dan, Jack and Howard were in the saloon, they saw Curt Jackson, the dust of a ride still upon him, walk in, cross to the bar and call for a beer. When he picked up the glass he strolled along the bar to join the three men.

'I've seen the Browns,' said Curt. 'You're in. Be upstairs at seven tonight.' He turned and walked away and Dan noticed that he paused at two tables to speak to cowboys before he hurried upstairs.

It was almost seven when Dan, accompanied by the Collins brothers, climbed the stairs in the saloon and knocked at the door of a room off the balcony. When they entered the room they found Curt Jackson and the rest of his gang already there.

Introductions over, Curt quickly outlined the plans for the coming raid. 'The Browns hev got word thet there will be twenty thousand dollars in the bank at Texola tomorrow. It will be there fer one night only – it's being shipped east by stage.'

'Why don't we bushwack the stage?' queried one of the men.

'Ed Brown learnt thet the stage is being heavily escorted an' he figures thet once thet money's in the bank the vigilance will relax somewhat,' explained Curt.

'What time are we pullin' this job?' asked Howard.

'About five,' replied the outlaw, 'just before the bank closes. Brown has hed the place looked over; there's few people usin' a bank at thet time of day an' the staff are weary after a day's work an' anxious to git off home.' He paused, reached for a drink, and studied the faces of the men around him. They were a tough, rugged bunch, and he figured the three newcomers would fit in well. 'We are not in on this alone,' continued Curt. 'The Browns reckon thet two more men will make the job safer, so they are ridin' with us themselves so you'll git all the final details when we meet up with them tomorrow at Granite. Usual procedure after the raid; split up if necessary; the Browns take the cash an' it will be distributed later, only this time it will be brought by some other hombre thet they hev with them.' He paused letting his words sink in before he asked, 'Any questions?'

The men shook their heads.

'All right,' said Jackson. 'Outside of here; seven in the mornin'.'

The following morning Curt Jackson led his gang out of Lone Wolf and kept to a brisk pace heading west until the small town of Granite came into sight. They swung north of the town until they reached a promontory overlooking the ill-kept shacks of the town. Jackson pulled his horse to a halt.

'We wait here,' he called as his men milled around him.

The gang swung from their saddles, thankful for the break. After securing their horses they stretched themselves on the ground, rolled themselves cigarettes, and awaited the arrival of Ed and Nick Brown. Ten minutes passed before they heard the clop of approaching horses. Immediately, they all jumped to their feet and Dan noticed that they all eased their Colts in the holsters, but relaxed when the two men came into sight.

Dan watched them with an eager curiosity, wondering how they compared with the two brothers he had killed. He noted that they rode easily, relaxed in their saddles, conserving their energy for what lay ahead. As they swung from the horses he noted that the tall, fair, broad-shouldered man did so with a casualness that belied the quickness of his movement and Dan figured that no matter how tight the corner he was in, he would still remain calm and unruffled.

'Howdy, boss,' greeted Curt.

Ed nodded to the outlaws as they grouped around him. His eyes rested on Jack and Howard and then passed to Dan who met the penetrating gaze with cold, blue eyes. Dan figured he was looking at a most dangerous man, who was cool, calculating and saw all the moves before anyone else.

'Glad you're in good time, Curt,' said Ed. 'These the new boys?'

'Yeah,' replied Curt and made the introductions.

Brown extended his hand to the three men. 'There's one thing to get straight now you've joined this outfit,' he said tersely. 'I'm the boss an' brother Nick is second in command; obey your instructions to the letter an' all will be well. We plan these raids in detail an' any deviation from the plan can wreck the whole thing. If we don't ride with you then you obey your section boss, in your case, Curt, without question. Play along right an' you'll be well rewarded.' He paused, letting his words sink in as he eyed the three newcomers. Suddenly he seemed to relax as if the three men had passed his scrutiny. 'All right,' he continued, his voice embracing all the gang who automatically shuffled nearer. 'Curt has told you about this raid, now we'll go into more detail.'

Ed Brown pulled a knife from his belt and traced two parallel lines on the ground. 'Thet's the main street in Texola,' he said. 'There's a short street at right angles to it about fifty yards from the bank, which is on the opposite side of the street, here.' He marked the position with a cross. 'You three new boys will position yourselves at thet corner. You other three,' he continued, glancing at Jackson's other men, 'will move further up the street on the same side as the bank. Nick, Curt an' I will git the cash.' He paused and glanced round the faces which had been watching him intently.

'Where's the sheriff's office?' asked one of the men.

'It's on your side of the bank, so keep your eyes open,' replied Brown.

The man nodded.

'If things go right,' continued Ed, 'we can git away without any shootin'. We figure on comin' out of thet bank as if we'd jest been in on business an' ride quietly out of Texola.

If we git away like that then you all follow in your own time. Don't rush it, an' don't all leave together. Any questions?'

'Where do we link up again?' asked Dan.

'We don't,' replied Brown. 'Make your own way back to Lone Wolf.'

'What about our share of the cash?' asked Howard.

'When you've ridden with the Browns,' drawled Nick dryly, 'you'll know you git fair dealings. Didn't you tell him, Curt?'

'Shore I did,' replied Jackson. 'I...'

'Thet's the least of your worries,' cut in Ed with a grin, 'but I suppose it's only natural you should wonder.'

'Suppose things don't go right?' asked Jack.

'Then it's your job to hold up any possible pursuit, an' then git away best you can,' replied Ed. 'But watch you aren't followed towards Lone Wolf. Now, if there are no more questions we'll git started.'

Wanting to conserve their horses' energy in case of a quick get-away, the Browns kept to a steady pace and it was mid-afternoon when Texola came into sight. The riders had reached the edge of some hills which fell gently to a flat stretch of country on which two miles away, lay the town.

77

'Wal, there it is,' called Ed, pulling his horse to a halt. 'There's twenty thousand dollars jest waitin' to be taken. We'll stay here an hour an' then drift into town.'

'Are we goin' to let them git away with this?' whispered Jack, as he sat down beside Dan.

'We're goin' to help them,' replied Dan without turning his head.

'But...' Jack started to protest, but Dan interrupted him.

'Our only chance to get near Babs is to play along with them; we've got to follow Brown back to their hide-out.'

'Supposin' things go wrong in town,' pointed out Jack, 'we're goin' to hev a hard time persuadin' the sheriff.'

'Thet's a chance we'll hev to take,' replied Dan. 'If we betray the Browns we could easily endanger Barbara's life.'

All further discussion stopped when two of the outlaws sat down close to them.

'Time to git movin!' The voice pierced Dan's mind, as he dozed, bringing him back to the reality of the pending raid. Cowboys stirred and pushed themselves to their feet to gather round Ed Brown.

'Ferguson, you and the Alvastons can ride into Texola now. Split before you reach town, but meet up on thet corner.' Ed turned to the other three outlaws. 'You can swing around the town an' come in from the other end. Curt, Nick, an' I will leave here in half an hour. Curt will enter the bank first an' if he doesn't reappear in ten seconds we know all is clear, then Nick an' I go in for the cash. Remember, take this easy like an' we can be away before any suspicion is aroused, so don't git itchy on those triggers.'

'How you goin to work this?' asked Dan.

'Thet's what we three are goin' over when you've hit the road to Texola,' replied Ed. 'But I can assure you thet, the way we've timed this, nobody in town need git any suspicions fer some time afterwards. All right, you can git ridin'.'

The group split up and Dan, accompanied by Jack and Howard, rode at a steady trot towards the small town of Texola.

'We'll split up before we reach town,' said Dan. 'I'll ride in alone, you two come in together. We'll take up our positions on opposite corners of the side street; I'll be on the one nearest the bank, so thet you'll hev me in view all the time, an' can take your cues from me.'

'Are you sure you're doin' the right thing, playin' along with this outfit?' asked How-

79

ard. 'Why not go to the law?'

'I prefer to do it this way; it's the only way we're likely to git a line of Babs,' replied Dan.

The two brothers realised it was useless to try to persuade Dan any more and the three men rode on in silence. A short distance out of town Dan pushed his horse ahead of the Collins brothers to reach Texola first.

Nearing the main street Dan slowed the pace, and in order to be as inconspicuous as possible, rode along the street at a walking pace. He studied its layout carefully before dismounting in front of the saloon. Hitching his horse to the rail he strolled casually on the sidewalk, pushed open the batwings, and sauntered across to the bar. As he sipped his beer, he noted that should trouble be forthcoming there would be little from that direction, as there were only four cowboys in the saloon. His thirst slaked, he left the building and as he unhitched his horse and pretended to adjust the saddle, he studied the bank, which was situated on the opposite side of the road. The entrance was on the corner of the building and from his position further along the street, Dan realised he would have a perfect view of the doorway. As he turned, he saw that the other three members of the gang had already taken up their positions and were lazing on the sidewalk opposite the sheriff's office. Dan led his horse along the street and hitched it to the rail outside the general store, which occupied the corner at which Ed Brown had instructed him to stand watch. He idled a few minutes, looking into the shop window, before turning to lean on the rail close to his horse. He glanced casually at the Collins brothers, who dismounted outside the café at the opposite corner of the side street. He saw them enter the café and seat themselves at a table in the window, from which they had a perfect view along the main street.

The minutes passed slowly, seeming an eternity to Dan. He realised it must be nearing closing time at the bank and still there was no sign of the Browns nor of Curt Jackson. Dan began to get anxious. Maybe something had caused Brown to change his plan and, if so, his contact with the Browns may have disappeared for the time being. He lit a cheroot but a few minutes later ground it out with his heel when he saw Curt Jackson riding into town.

The outlaw showed no signs of recognition as he passed him and, as Curt dismounted in front of the bank, Dan saw the Brown

81

brothers were already riding down Main Street. Curt took his time about hitching his horse to the rail and moved towards the bank only when the Browns were about fifty yards away. The brothers swung from the saddles in front of the bank and, as Curt had not reappeared, they strolled into the building.

Dan glanced towards the café and saw that Jack and Howard were on the sidewalk. A tenseness seemed to hang in the air, but Dan realised it was only his imagination! Texola was quietly going through a normal afternoon.

Suddenly, the door of the bank opened and Ed and Nick Brown crossed the sidewalk to their horses, flung the bags they were carrying across the animals' backs, climbed into the saddles and put the horses into a steady trot out of town. Dan stared anxiously at the doorway. Where was Curt? A man crossed the street towards the bank! Dan stiffened, his hand moving closer to his holster, but the man turned and walked along the sidewalk. A movement in the doorway attracted Dan's attention. Curt was bolting and locking the doors.

The cleverness and audacity of the plan suddenly made its impact upon Dan. By timing the raid for the last minute before the bank closed, the outlaws were able to lock up and with the cashiers and manager either dead or unconscious inside, no one would be likely to suspect that anything was wrong until they were missed.

A few moments passed before Curt, who had left the bank by a side door, emerged from an alley and strolled casually to his horse. He climbed into the saddle and rode at a walking pace in the same direction as the Browns.

Dan waited a few minutes, leaning on the rail, until he saw Curt had already reached the edge of town. He straightened from the rail and walked towards Jack and Howard. As he did so, two men passed so close to him that Dan could not help overhearing their remarks.

'Good place for the meeting,' said one.

'Yeah,' agreed the other. 'Brightwell said he would leave the front door open for five minutes.'

The two men stepped down from the sidewalk and Dan gasped when he realised they were heading for the bank. He looked quickly along the street, but the three outlaws who had been watching the sheriff's office were already riding out of town in the opposite direction to that taken by the Browns.

83

Dan hurried to Jack and Howard.

'Two hombres headin' for the bank,' said Dan nodding towards the two men, who were already stepping on to the opposite sidewalk.

'Then the hold-up will be discovered sooner than Brown expected,' gasped Jack.

'What we goin' to do?' asked Howard.

'Not much we can do on our own,' replied Dan. 'Jest hang on an' see what develops.'

The two men who were already trying the door to the bank looked amazed when they found it locked. They hurried to the alley and a few moments later Dan saw the front door flung open and the two men, surprise and panic showing on their faces, rushed from the building.

'Get the Doc,' yelled one to a passer-by and ran across the road to the sheriff's office.

The other looked up and down the street and hurried to two ladies who had been standing together on the side walk for some considerable time. As the man approached them Dan hurried across the street.

'Did you see anyone come out of the bank recently?' Dan heard him ask the two ladies.

'Yes,' they both agreed, 'two men rode off in that direction and a few minutes later another went the same way, but we didn't see him come out of the bank; he came out of the alley.'

'Thanks,' cried the man. 'Bank's been robbed, manager and cashier hurt, the doc might need a hand.' He turned and almost bumped into Dan. 'You see them, young fellah?'

'Shore,' Dan replied, realising it was no use denying the ladies' observations.

As the man dashed along the street towards the sheriff, who was running along the street followed by several other men, Dan followed.

'Three men were seen headin' thet way,' he called as he reached the sheriff.

'Good,' answered the sheriff. 'Git your horses, bring mine, Eb. I'll see if I can git a description.' He turned towards the bank, but stopped when he saw Dan.

'Stranger round here?' he asked suspiciously.

'Shore,' replied Dan. 'Saw them hombres leave the bank. Me an' my two buddies jest passin' through. If you're raisin' a posse we'll ride.'

The offer convinced the sheriff. 'Good,' he said, and hurried into the bank. He re-appeared a few moments later and swung

85

into the saddle of his horse.

'Description fits the Browns,' he shouted as the posse milled around. 'Got away with thet special shipment.' He kicked his horse into a gallop and the posse thundered away from Texola.

Chapter Seven

Curt Jackson, feeling well satisfied with the way things had gone, put his horse into a fast trot once he was clear of Texola. Some considerable distance ahead, he could see the Brown brothers pushing their horses at a fast pace towards the hills.

He was tempted to quicken his pace to catch up to them, but to do so would have been to disobey the instructions laid down by Ed Brown. Curt was to hang behind to give warning should there be any pursuit. He grinned to himself, thinking that Ed stretched his precautions too far. There had been no firing back in Texola, so everything must have gone according to plan and the rest of the gang must have left the town by now.

Jackson pushed his horse hard as the ground rose steadily towards the first ridge over which the Browns had disappeared.

When he reached the top of the rise he pulled his horse to a halt and glanced back towards Texola. Startled, he stiffened in his saddle, hardly able to believe his eyes. A group of horsemen raised the dust as they headed away from town at a fast gallop. Curt jerked his horse round and kicked it forward. What had gone wrong? He had heard no shots. How had the robbery been discovered so quickly? His brain pounded with questions as he galloped after the Browns. As soon as he saw them he pulled his Colt from its holster and fired two shots into the air. He saw the brothers pause momentarily, wave their acknowledgement, and then put their horses into a fast gallop.

Curt kept to his brisk pace until the trail dropped into a cutting and forked at the junction of two shallow valleys. He pulled his horse to a sliding halt when he saw that the Browns, who had taken the left fork as arranged, were already out of sight. He glanced behind, and, when he saw that the pursuers had not yet crossed the ridge, he surveyed his immediate surroundings quickly. Noticing a group of rocks half way up the hillside to his right, he decided to use them as cover, and, if necessary, draw the lawmen away from the direction taken by the Brown brothers.

It was not long before the pound of hoofs heralded the approach of hard-ridden horses. Curt gasped when the riders came into view and he saw Dan, together with Jack and Howard, riding close to the sheriff.

'The low-down...' he muttered to himself. His eyes narrowed and glared with a hate which bore the three men no good, should he ever come face to face with them.

The posse brought their horses to a halt at the fork and milled around the sheriff. Curt tensed himself behind the rocks waiting for Dan to point out the pre-arranged trail taken by the Browns.

'Up there! They've just crossed thet ridge!' Dan shouted suddenly, pointing along the right hand valley.

This deliberate misleading of the posse surprised Curt, and he watched the men wheel their horses and send them at a fast gallop along the valley. As their hoofs pounded into the distance and they disappeared from view, Curt smiled to himself.

'Smart work, Ferguson,' he muttered. 'How you come to be with thet lot, I don't know, but you've shore fooled them.'

Jackson swung into the saddle and set out for Lone Wolf.

Dan cursed at the early discovery of the robbery, but the only way to throw suspicion from himself and his companions, as they were strangers in Texola, was to fall in with the sheriff and ride with the posse.

As they pounded out of Texola Dan was troubled, for he saw the chance of following the Browns and getting close to Barbara diminishing. Somehow or other they must throw the sheriff off the pursuit, give the posse the slip, and get back on the trail of the Browns themselves.

As they galloped across the flat country out of Texola they saw the distant figures heading into the hills. The sheriff called for a faster pace, but Dan realised that the outlaws could easily give them the slip once they were across the first ridge. He hoped they would follow their pre-arranged route otherwise the plan he had in mind could easily go astray.

Hopefully the posse thundered into the hills to pull to a halt at a fork in the trail, but Dan quickly directed them to the right, unaware that his action had been observed by Curt Jackson.

Once they climbed out of the valley on to the ridge, and they saw no sign of the men they were pursuing, the sheriff called a halt.

'Are you sure you saw them?' he asked.

'Yes,' replied Dan.

'Guess we'd better spread out,' instructed the lawman. 'Two shots if you see them.'

Dan grinned to himself. This was exactly what he had hoped for. He nodded to the Collins brothers and they moved to the left as the rest of the posse split up. Once they were out of sight of the other men they turned their horses to cut across the hills to the trail taken by the Browns. Dan, anxious to make contact with the outlaws again, pushed the pace hard, but after an hour's riding he had to admit that they had no chance of seeing them.

'Guess it's no use,' he said gloomily. 'They must hev known about the posse an' left this trail. May as well head for Lone Wolf.'

'Thing's aren't hopeless,' Jack reassured him. 'We can trail this hombre after he's delivered the cash to Curt.'

As darkness was closing across the country-side, the three men decided to camp for the night. They were in the saddles before sun-up the following day and by mid-morning they were dismounting in front of the saloon in Lone Wolf. Pushing through the batwings they crossed to the bar.

'Jackson in?' asked Dan.

The barman nodded towards the stairs and the three men climbed them quickly and were soon greeted by the call of 'Come in' when they rapped on the door of Jackson's room.

'Howdy,' greeted Dan.

Curt nodded and eyed the three men carefully before fixing his gaze on Dan.

'Why were you ridin' with thet posse?' he asked coldly.

Dan was caught off his guard, but he controlled his expression and quickly explained the happenings in Texola.

Curt listened intently and, as Dan finished, a grin spread across his face. 'This is rich,' he laughed, slapping his thigh. 'We hold up a bank an' part of the gang rides with the posse. The Browns will shore be tickled with this one. Thet was a mighty quick bit of thinkin', Ferguson, an' a good move at the fork – thet's where I saw you.'

Throughout the days which followed, McCoy and the Collins brothers kept watch for a stranger who tried to contact Jackson. After the fourth day Dan was beginning to get a little uneasy and decided to scout around the hills, leaving Jack and Howard to keep watch in town. It was late afternoon when, after a fruitless search, he was riding back to Lone Wolf and failed to notice a horseman on the ridge above him. The man watched Dan through narrowing eyes. There was something familiar about the man who rode towards Lone Wolf. The rider spurred his horse forward to bring it nearer the trail ahead of Dan. From the corner of a group of rocks the man watched Dan approaching at an easy pace.

Suddenly he stiffened. 'McCoy!' he gasped in surprise. He pulled his rifle from its leather and took careful aim. As the crash of the rifle reverberated round the rocks Dan's horse reared with fright, flinging him from the saddle as the bullet crashed into his shoulder. He hit the ground on the edge of a steep slope and stones and earth tumbled after him as he rolled faster and faster down the slope until he plunged into the river.

As soon as he saw he had hit Dan, the cowboy spurred his horse forward to the edge of the trail and grinned with satisfaction when he saw Dan roll into the river. Joe Burgess waited a moment and, when he saw that McCoy did not come to the surface, he turned his horse and put it into a trot along the trail.

The sudden shock of the cold water cleared Dan's brain. He kept below the surface and when his aching lungs, bursting for air, forced him upwards he was thankful that he had been able to stay underwater, for now the man was riding away. He reached for the bank and dragged himself out of the water. His shoulder was painful, but when he examined it he was thankful that he had received nothing worse than a flesh wound. After climbing the slope and retrieving his horse, he made his way back to Lone Wolf.

He dismounted outside the dilapidated hotel and hurried upstairs, glad to find both Jack and Howard in their room.

'What happened?' Anxiety showed in their voices as Dan walked in and they saw his bloodstained shirt.

Dan told his story, whilst Howard and Jack tended to the wound.

'Could it hev been that hombre we followed from here?' said Jack, looking at his brother when Dan had finished.

'He's been?' said Dan excitedly, as he eased his clean shirt over the wound.

'Yeah,' replied Howard, but the glum look on his face foretold Dan that all had not gone well. 'This hombre arrived; Jack an' I were in the saloon. We saw him go up to Curt Jackson's room and when he reappeared about half an hour later we followed him out of Lone Wolf, but we lost him in the hills. We tried to pick up his trail again, but

I'm afraid we were out of luck. Sorry, Dan.'

Disappointment showed on McCoy's face. 'It can't be helped,' he said, shrugging his shoulders. 'You did your best. We'll jest hev to wait fer somethin' else to turn up.'

'Could be the same hombre thet shot you,' said Jack.

'Why should he take a shot at Dan?' queried Howard.

'Maybe, he recognised him?' suggested Jack.

'Did you know him?' asked Dan.

The brothers shook their heads. 'No, I can't say we did,' answered Jack.

'More likely saw I was a stranger around these parts, an' you know how touchy the Browns are about strangers,' said Dan. 'Wal, it doesn't git us any nearer Barbara. When do we meet Curt fer the pay-off?'

'To-night at seven-thirty,' replied Howard.

As Joe Burgess rode into Browns' camp, Nick greeted him. 'You look mighty pleased with yourself, everything must hev gone well.'

'Shore did,' answered Joe. 'Delivered the cash an' I've disposed of Dan McCoy fer you!'

'What!' Ed and Nick gasped at the news.

'No!' Barbara screamed as she jumped to her feet. Her hands were clenched tightly against her mouth, her eyes were wide with horror, as she stared at Burgess.

The men ignored her and Joe told his story. The rest of the outlaws congratulated him when he had finished, and Barbara sank to the ground, her body shaking as sobs racked her.

It was during the evening meal that the question of Barbara arose.

'What are we goin' to do with her now?' Nick asked Ed, nodding towards Barbara who merely picked at the plate of stew.

'I've been thinkin' about thet,' replied Ed. 'We hev a chance to move into Red Springs now. Joe's talked about the Bar X, wal, I'll pay a visit to lawyer Saunders on the way so we can take it over all legal like.'

'How are you goin' to work thet?' asked Nick.

Ed chuckled to himself and went on to discuss his plan with his brother and the three members of his gang.

'As owners of the Bar X,' he finished, 'we can operate the countryside around Red Springs under the cover of respectability, and, at the same time, take our revenge on old man Collins an' his sons as well as deputy sheriff Schofield fer the part they played in killin' our brothers.'

'Smart thinkin',' congratulated Nick. 'But what about her?'

'We'll take her along in case anythin' goes wrong,' replied Ed. A grin spread across his face. 'Imagine old man Collins if we confront him with his daughter!'

Chapter Eight

As they rode through the Wichita Mountains, Barbara was not aware of the direction they were taking. Her brain was numb with the horror of Dan's shooting. When Joe Burgess had ridden in with the news she longed for Brown to kill her, but only his scrupulous attention to detail, his flair for taking every precaution, had kept her alive.

The horses' hooves thrummed on the ground and slowly the words Red Springs beat into Barbara's brain to the rhythm of the ride. The constant pound of the words brought her back to reality. Even if Dan was dead she could not let the Browns take revenge on her father and brothers. She must do something to warn them. Her brain began to clear and she began to look for some means of escape. She realised she must not betray any sign of alertness to the men around her and continued to ride limp in the saddle. The miles flashed past, under the pounding hooves, but the riders held to their positions and no opportunity to escape presented itself.

It was late in the day when Ed Brown called a halt, about five miles from the Red River, between Oklahoma and Texas.

The men were pleased to be out of the saddle and Barbara slid wearily to the ground. They made camp quickly, and, after a satisfying meal, the party prepared to settle down for the night. Mart Webster strolled to Barbara who, lost in her own thoughts, had sat apart from the men. She didn't stir as the man stopped in front of her.

'I've to tie you up,' he said. 'We are safe enough in this part of the country so there are no guards on tonight.'

Barbara stared sullenly at him, her eyes clouded with hate and anger. She knew it was useless to object, so she extended her hands as the outlaw bent down. He tied her wrists together and then swiftly wound a piece of rope round her ankles. Barbara's head sank against her saddle as he turned to go.

'You might throw a blanket over me,' she said.

Without a word the outlaw spread two blankets over her before going to his own bed roll. Weariness and delayed shock suddenly became overpowering in the silence of the Oklahoma night; Barbara felt frightened and alone. Tears flowed freely as sobs racked her body. Sleep came slowly and then only fitfully, but gradually Barbara began to think again of escape.

She was thankful that the man had not been too particular when he had tied her up. The ropes were secure enough, but the fact that she had extended her arms towards him seemed to have made him forget that she would have been more helpless had he tied her arms behind her back. Now she was able to reach forward and unfasten the rope around her ankles.

Once her legs were free she paused and looked round the camp, but all was still; her movements had disturbed no one. She turned her attention to the rope round her wrists, pulling and tugging in the attempt to free her hands, but it was no use. The rope was too tight. She looked round desperately and was tempted to make a run for it as she was, but realised it would be useless; she could not saddle her horse with her hands tied, and to go on foot would be of no use.

Barbara raised her hands to wipe her brow and as she did so the realisation that she had the means to undo the rope suddenly struck her. Excitedly, she closed her teeth on the rope and pulled at it desperately. She tugged hard, but the rope did not yield. In spite of the chill in the night air, sweat broke out on her forehead as she jerked her head backwards and forwards, pulling at the rope. She felt as if her teeth would be pulled from her mouth, but still she kept up her efforts to free herself. Her persistence was rewarded when she felt the rope give slightly. Eagerly her teeth fastened tighter on the rope and inch by inch the knot came undone. Excitedly, she fastened on to the second knot and it seemed an eternity before it yielded to her efforts, and she was able to fling the rope aside. She massaged her wrists vigorously, until the circulation was restored, then she lay down and carefully studied the camp.

The men were sleeping soundly, but she realised that in order to reach the horses she would have to pass close to two of the silent forms. Throwing the blankets off she rose silently to her feet and arranged the clothes so that it would appear as if she was still sleeping. She picked up her saddle and slowly made her way towards the horses. As she crept across the camp the saddle seemed to weigh heavier and heavier until she felt as if she must drop it. Desperately she clutched it tighter and moved even more cautiously as she neared two sleeping cowboys. Suddenly she froze in her tracks, hardly daring to breathe. One of the men stirred and turned over! Barbara remained where she was until she was certain he was still asleep. She reached the picket line without further alarm and was relieved to see her horse was at the end. She whispered soothingly to the animal and hoped that her presence would not disturb the others.

Carefully she laid the blanket and saddle across the horse's back and soon had them secured. She untied the horse and led it gently away from the camp. The desire to hurry was strong, but she knew it would be fatal to make a sound and so she made her way patiently until she felt safe enough to mount. She kept the animal to a walking pace for about half a mile before putting it into a trot and finally into a gallop towards the Red River.

Dawn was streaking the eastern horizon with the first light when Ed Brown stirred. Through eyes still half-closed with sleep, he automatically glanced in the direction of his prisoner. There was no movement; she appeared to be fast asleep. Brown turned, flung the blankets to one side, pushed himself to his feet and stretched, driving the ache of sound sleep from his body. He picked up his gun belt and as he fastened it round his hips, he roused the rest of the gang.

In spite of his shouts there was still no movement from the girl. He crossed towards her, but suddenly stopped momentarily. There was no saddle! He jumped forward pulling the blankets back. His eyes widened when he saw no one there.

'She's gone!' he yelled, spinning round to face his men. 'Mart, you tied her up. What the…?'

'Sorry boss,' apologised Mart. 'I thought she was…'

'Never mind mumbling excuses now, get after her; her horse has gone,' he yelled, pointing to the line of horses.

In a matter of minutes the horses were saddled, camp broken, and the men following the signs of Barbara's movements. Progress was slow and when they reached the point where Barbara had mounted her horse Ed Brown decided to take a gamble.

'Tracks lead thet way,' he pointed out. 'Reckon she's headed for the Red River.'

'Could hev deviated,' replied Nick.

'Maybe, but at this rate we won't catch

her,' said Ed. 'We'll head fer the river fast.' Without waiting for further comment he kicked his horse into a gallop and the others followed suit, keeping close on his heels.

They covered the ground quickly and when they reached the final ridge, from which there was a long gentle slope to the river, the men pulled to a halt and scanned the countryside.

'There she is!' yelled Joe Burgess, pointing to a lone rider, who hurried close to the water, searching for a suitable crossing.

The five men spurred their horses and earth flew as hoofs pounded the ground in full gallop.

It was light by the time Barbara sighted the Red River. Realising that her flight could have been discovered, and that by now the Browns would be searching for her, she drove her horse harder towards the river, only to rein hard when she saw the swirling waters. This was no place to cross! She must find a ford quickly. Desperately she turned her horse along the bank.

Barbara had only ridden a short distance when she heard the distant pound of hoofs. The alarm which showed in her eyes when she glanced round changed to fear when she saw the five horsemen galloping in her direction. She kicked her horse into a gallop, her eyes searching ahead for some means of crossing the river, but all she could see was fast, swirling water.

The men were closing the distance rapidly, and she saw that two of them were already moving ahead and cutting across her path.

Barbara jerked hard on the reins bringing the horse to an earth-tearing, sliding halt. She pulled the animal round, but saw that two other men had moved behind her and Ed Brown was riding straight towards her. Fear showed on her face. She looked anxiously at the river, swirling and rushing past, and in one desperate moment made her decision. She pulled the horse round sharply towards the water. The animal hesitated, but Barbara kicked it hard and sent it plunging bravely into the grey, grasping water.

It struck out from the bank strongly and Barbara praised it with encouraging words, but soon the pull of the swirling waters began to tell and their progress became slower. The girl slipped from the saddle to relieve the animal of some weight, and holding on to the stirrup called on the horse for greater effort. The animal responded and gradually they drew further and further from the bank, but when they reached midstream Barbara suddenly felt much of the power go out of the horse and the river take command.

As they were swept downstream, Barbara realised that as long as the horse had some strength she must hold on to the stirrup, for she would have little chance in the rushing water on her own. The river spun and twisted them as it swept them downstream; one moment Barbara was plunged under the surface, the next she was gasping for air.

As he watched her from the bank, Nick Brown could not but admire the bravery of the girl as she made her desperate bid to escape. Suddenly he stiffened when he saw the horse lose strength.

He turned his horse sharply and galloped hard along the bank, unfastening his lariat as he did so. Once he was slightly ahead of Barbara he stopped, and swinging the lariat around his head sent it curling high across the water. Although it was only a matter of seconds, it seemed an eternity to Nick, before he saw the rope fall neatly over the horse's head. Swiftly he wound the rope round his saddle and as it tightened round the animal's neck he took the strain, calling strongly to his own horse. Gradually the animal responded to his shouts and backed away from the water's edge. Inch by inch, foot by foot, it moved, straining against the tug of the powerful water. As the rest of the gang thundered along the bank of the river, Mart Webster drew alongside Nick and his lariat curled across the water to fall over the horse's head. The extra help soon had the animal moving towards the bank, in spite of the dragging, clutching water.

Barbara's arm ached as the strain began to tell. She felt as if it would be torn from its socket, and already she was on the point of not caring whether she was saved or not. Ten yards from the bank her hand began to slip and in the relaxation the river seemed to tug harder. Her fingers slipped slowly round the stirrup, then suddenly it was gone.

Ed Brown, who had moved close to the water's edge, had seen what was happening and as Barbara's hand slipped, he threw his rope. It fell around the girl's shoulders, and as it tightened Ed pulled hard. Joe Burgess jumped from the saddle and leaped to Ed's side to help him pull Barbara from the water. Eager hands dragged her on to the bank, where she lay gasping for breath until blackness flooded in and she fainted with exhaustion.

When Barbara regained consciousness she found Ed Brown kneeling beside her forcing brandy between her lips. As her brain cleared she struggled to sit up.

'Thet's better,' said Brown. 'Thet shore was a fool thing to do. Maybe we should hev let you drown.' He straightened to his feet and looked down at the girl. 'But I might need you in Red Springs.' Despair filled Barbara as he turned away. 'Joe, git a fire goin' down amongst those trees,' he ordered. 'Mrs McCoy'll dry out whilst the rest of you find some place to cross this river.'

The men split up and Barbara, with Joe's saddle blanket around her, was soon drying her clothes in front of a fire. By the time she was ready Nick, Mart and Wally had returned to report that they had found a ford five miles up stream.

As they mounted their horses Ed warned Barbara. 'Don't try anything again.' His voice was coldly threatening. 'Next time I may hev to kill you.'

The rest of the journey was uneventful and it was early evening when they found a suitable place to camp, five miles out of Red Springs.

'We'll stay here the night,' said Ed. 'And there'll be a guard all night, Mrs McCoy –

we can't hev you escaping so near to Red Springs. Tomorrow Nick an' I will give this town a surprise.'

The following morning Ed and Nick Brown rode slowly into Red Springs and dismounted in front of the sheriff's office. They knocked on the door and walked in, to find Clint Schofield seated behind the desk.

'You the sheriff?' asked Ed pleasantly.

'Nope,' replied Clint. 'Sheriff's out of town. I'm his deputy. Anythin' I can do fer you?'

'Wal,' drawled Ed, 'thought we'd introduce ourselves; Pete Young, brother Bert; an' ask you to direct us to our ranch – the Bar X.'

'Bar X!' Clint stared incredulously at the two strangers. 'But thet's Bill Collins' spread.'

Ed looked disbelievingly at Clint. 'Can't be. We bought it from a man by the name of Wayman. Seems his brother was killed an' the ranch left to him. He didn't want to leave the east so he sold it to us.'

'But Bill Collins brought it from him,' protested Clint.

'What!' cried Nick. 'Seems somebody's been taken fer a ride. Said I didn't trust thet old coot.'

Clint eyed the two men coldly. 'You've got a bill of sale, I presume,' he said.

'Shore,' answered Ed.

'Then I reckon we'd better pay a visit to Bob Walker, our lawyer, an' git this thing straightened out.'

Bob Walker was as surprised as Clint when he was confronted with the news. He examined the bill of sale which Ed had had drawn up by a crooked lawyer before leaving Oklahoma.

'This isn't Wayman's signature,' he said suspiciously.

'Shore it isn't,' answered Ed. 'He got a lawyer to do the transaction. Thet's his signature.'

Bob examined the document again. 'M'm, the seal seems genuine enough. Reckon it's all right, Clint,' he said.

'But who does the Bar X belong to?' queried Clint, not knowing what to make of the situation.

'Wal, this document bears a date earlier than thet I hold fer Bill Collins,' explained Bob, 'so I reckon the Bar X had already been sold to these two gentlemen before it was sold to Bill.'

Clint took off his sombrero and scratched his head, a puzzled expression on his face. 'Bill shore is in fer a surprise,' he said. 'He ain't goin' to like it. Guess I'd better ride out with you fellahs.'

The three men left the office and were soon riding at a steady pace towards the Bar X.

As they neared the long, low ranch-house, a man came on to the veranda.

'Hello, Bill,' greeted Clint as he pulled to a halt in front of the buildings.

'Mornin', Clint,' answered Bill Collins. He nodded to the other two riders. 'Any news from Dan?' he asked hopefully.

The three men swung from the saddles, and as Clint walked on to the veranda he shook his head. 'Sorry, Bill, I haven't, an' I'm afraid I'm bringin' you more bad news.'

Bill's face clouded with concern. 'What's wrong?' he asked.

'Let me introduce Pete Young an' Bert Young,' said Clint. 'They reckon they're the real owners of the Bar X.'

'What!' gasped Collins. 'They can't be. I bought the spread.'

'Seems it was bought twice,' explained Clint, 'an' their bill of sale is dated before yours.'

Collins stared incredulously at the three men. 'We'd better see what Bob Walker has to say about this.'

'I've already seen him,' replied Clint. 'Bob says thet the bill of sale seems genuine enough.'

Collins stared at the three men, hardly able to realise what was happening to him. His brain was numb. The Bar X, which he had built up since taking it over after the Pickering brothers had been exposed, was slipping away from him. It couldn't happen to him.

'You can't get away with this!' he screamed suddenly.

His hand flashed towards his holster, but Clint, sensing what would happen, was already on the move. He leaped forward, grabbing Bill's hand as it closed round the butt of the gun.

'Thet's not the way, Bill,' yelled Clint as the two men staggered backwards under the weight of the impact.

'Let me at those two coyotes,' shouted Collins, struggling to free himself from the deputy sheriff.

Clint's grip tightened. He saw Bill's eyes blazing with anger, the wildness of some cheated animal in them. Quickly he brought his right hand upwards, crashing his fist into the rancher's face. Collins staggered backwards and fell in the dust. His eyes half shut then widened with surprise. Clint, who tensed himself over Collins, saw that his eyes were clear, the wildness had gone from them. Slowly Collins sat up, feeling his jaw tenderly. He pushed himself to his feet and looked sheepishly at Clint.

'Sorry, old friend,' he apologised. 'I should hev known better.'

'Thet's all right, Bill,' said Clint, patting Collins on the arm. 'I'm sorry I hed to do thet.'

Ed stepped forward. 'I guess this is pretty hard on you,' he said. 'Wayman said there was a client in Red Springs, but when he accepted our ready cash we naturally thought he would let you know – not take your money as well.'

Collins shook his head sadly. 'Guess there's not much I can do about it right away,' he said. 'In any case, I've little chance of catchin' up with Wayman; he'll hev moved on by now.'

'Seems you caught the wrong end of the stick,' said Clint. 'I'd never hev thought John Wayman would hev hed a crooked brother.'

'When do you want me out?' asked Collins, turning to Ed.

'Wal, thet's up to you,' replied Ed amiably.

'Thet's mighty kind of you,' said Bill. 'I reckon I can be clear of here in two days. I'll hev to move back on to the Circle C, Clint,' he continued, turning to the deputy sheriff.

113

'I don't like doin' it when I gave it to Barbara an' especially when she isn't...' His voice trailed away. He turned and walked sadly into the house.

'Been a rough time fer him,' said Clint, as the three men went to their horses. 'His daughter's disappeared; we reckon she might hev been kidnapped. Her husband an' her two brothers hev ridden north hoping to pick up some lead, but we hevn't heard a word from them.'

'Too bad,' said Nick, as he swung into the saddle. 'If there's anythin' we can do let us know.'

'Thanks,' said Clint. 'You fellahs ride back on your own. I think I'll stay with Bill fer a while.'

The brothers nodded and, with a wave to Clint, put their horses into a fast trot away from the Bar X. Their faces were broken by grins of smug satisfaction at the accomplishment of the first part of their plan.

Chapter Nine

Two days later a weary, worried Bill Collins rode into Red Springs and swung from the saddle in front of the hotel.

'Howdy, Bill,' greeted the proprietor as Collins entered the lobby.

'Hello, Jeb,' answered Bill, his voice flat, without sparkle. 'Hev you two hombres name of Pete an' Bert Young stayin' here?'

'Yes,' answered Jeb, 'but they've jest gone to the saloon.'

'Thanks,' replied Bill and left the hotel.

He walked across the street, pushed through the batwings of the saloon and paused to survey the room, which was half full of cowboys, saloon girls, and local towns-people. Bill's gaze froze on a table when he saw Pete Young, Bert Young, and four prominent citizens of Red Springs.

'They've lost no time in getting to know the right people,' muttered Bill to himself, as he walked towards the table, noticing that the four men seemed to be already on inti-mate terms with the newcomers.

'Collins!' called the elder brother as Bill approached. 'Mighty glad to see you. Hev a drink.' He called to the barman for another glass.

'Howdy, Bill,' greeted the others.

'Too bad about the Bar X,' sympathised one.

'Seems you were taken in,' said another.

Collins, his face showing no pleasure, nodded a greeting to them all.

'I hevn't seen you since your visit to the Bar X,' he said addressing the man he knew as Pete Young. 'Thought I'd better ride in an' let you know I'm clear of it now.'

'Thanks,' grinned Ed amiably, 'but you needn't hev rushed.' He poured a drink from the bottle on the table and offered it to Bill. 'Take a seat,' he said.

Bill accepted the drink, but refused the chair. 'Hevn't time,' he said. 'Got somethin' to attend to.'

'You should,' said one of the men, 'an' hear what our new neighbours hev in mind fer Red Springs.'

Collins looked at him curiously.

'Yeah,' said another enthusiastically. 'We've been half asleep all these years. The Youngs, here, hev schemes to put Red Springs on the map – there's a fortune to be made if we follow them up.'

'Things hev been all right fer years,' replied Collins. 'You hev all been content with what you've had. We've all been makin' nice livin's an' Red Springs has been kept a respectable, peace-lovin' town.'

'An' there's no need fer it to change,' came the reply. 'You haven't even heard what their proposals are,' he added, when he saw Bill eye him doubtfully.

'No, an' I don't want to,' snapped Bill. His voice rose. 'You don't know anythin' about these two men. They come here, strangers, you listen to them an' fall fer their schemes, you who've been here most of your lives an' hev reached important positions in this town. They're foxin' you with smart talk, but mark my words, it will be only for their own ends. There's something fishy about this Bar X business. I've moved off on Clint Schofield's advice, but I'm enquirin' into the claim.' He looked hard at Ed; his eyes narrowed, burning with anger; his voice lowered but lashed at the man. 'An' if I find you're on a crooked deal I'll come gunnin' fer you myself!'

Nick's hand moved towards his holster, but Ed put out a restraining hand. He tilted his chair backwards swinging on the back

117

two legs. A sarcastic grin crossed his face as he looked at Collins.

'I'm afraid we're here to stay, Collins,' he said. 'You'll hev to git used to it. I understand from my new friends here thet you are a man of some standing around here. Now if you don't come in with us, wal, I guess it won't be long before you're jest small fry.'

'Don't be hasty in your decision, Bill,' advised one of the men from Red Springs. 'You're bound to feel sore about the Bar X, but here's a chance to make some of thet money back. I'll come over an' see you tomorrow an' put the scheme to you.'

'You needn't bother,' rasped Bill. 'I'm makin' enquiries about these two,' an' it's my bet they're not what they appear to be. If they are, then I'll apologise an' listen to your scheme.'

'It might be too late then,' said Ed coldly.

Collins spun on his heel without a word and left the saloon. He crossed the street and walked down the sidewalk to his horse.

Depressed and worried he felt the need to talk to someone and rode along the street towards the neat, trim houses which lay at the west end of the main street. As he passed the sheriff's office, he saw a light through the window. Pulling his horse to a halt he slipped from the saddle and walked into the office where he found Clint Schofield cleaning his Colt.

'No news from Dan yet?' he asked as he closed the door.

Clint shook his head. 'Sorry,' he replied.

Collins shrugged his shoulders. 'Looks bad,' he said quietly.

'Don't give up hope,' answered Clint, trying to sound enthusiastic. 'Everythin' seems to be goin' wrong at once, but it will come out right in the end.'

'From what I've jest heard, Clint, trouble is comin' to Red Springs,' said Collins. 'I was on my way to see Bob Walker when I saw the light in here, you'd better come along too.'

'Jest as you wish,' answered Clint, picking up his Stetson. He knew it was useless to press Collins any further at the moment, so he followed him out of the office and the two men walked to Bob Walker's house in silence.

Their knock was answered by a smart, middle-aged woman.

'Good evenin', Joan,' said Bill, touching his Stetson 'Is Bob in?'

'Hello, Bill,' greeted Mrs Walker. 'Clint. Come in both of you.'

The two men stepped inside the lighted hall. Mrs Walker closed the door and as she turned and saw Bill Collins, the warm smile changed to one of shocked surprise.

'Bill Collins,' she admonished. 'You're letting things get on top of you. I know you're having a lot of worry at the moment, but Barbara wouldn't like to see you like this. You want a good rest, or you won't be able to fight for your rights, and you look as though you could do with a good feed. I'll bet you haven't had a square meal since this trouble blew up.'

A faint smile flickered across Bill's face. 'Never try to hide anythin' from a woman, Clint.'

'I knew I was right,' went on Mrs Walker. 'Now, whilst you're talkin' to Bob, I'll get you a meal ready; you'll stay too Clint?'

Clint nodded. 'Thanks,' he said.

'Hello Bill, Clint,' greeted Bob Walker, when his wife showed them into a room.

'Sorry to bother you at home,' said Bill, 'but I figured you an' Clint ought to hear what I've jest heard in the saloon.'

Bob looked at Bill curiously, indicated chairs, offered them both a cheroot, and when they were all comfortably settled, Collins told his story.

'There's not a lot to go on,' said Bob, as he finished.

'A pity you didn't listen to their schemes,' said Clint.

'Guess so,' said Bill, 'but I was so upset about the Bar X an' then to see these two strangers talkin' about schemes fer a fortune in Red Springs, I jest didn't want to listen.'

'There's not much we can do at the moment except keep our eyes an' ears open,' said Bob. 'After all, they're not breakin' the law.'

'How long will it take to check on their claim to the Bar X?' asked Collins.

'About a month,' replied Walker.

'Then get on to it right away,' said Bill. 'I think you'll find somethin' strange about it. In the meantime, we'll hev to watch out an' try and get into this idea of theirs; they seemed to be prepared to offer me a share in it.'

Bob and Clint agreed, and after an enjoyable meal Bill left the house feeling much better.

It was a pleasant night, starlit and calm, and Bill rode at a slow trot towards the Circle C. A group of small, low hillocks broke the trail ahead at a point where it was crossed by a cattle trail running north and

121

south towards the Bar X and Wayman's Ford.

As he approached the crossing, Bill stiffened in the saddle. He pulled his horse to a halt and listened intently. A dull, distant pound reached his ears and as it grew louder he recognised it as hard-ridden horses moving along the trail from his left. Bill Collins hurried forward and took up a position from which he could see the crossing clearly without being seen. As the thrum of pounding hoofs grew louder, Bill knew that several horses were being ridden in urgent gallop. Suddenly they were in view and almost as quickly had vanished into the night in the direction of the Bar X and Wayman's Ford.

Collins had recognised Bert Young, tall in the saddle, and guessed Pete Young had been leading the party.

'Must've hed their cowpokes camped pretty close all the time,' he muttered to himself. 'They certainly seemed sure of themselves.' He rode slowly along the trail. 'Six of them,' he whispered. 'Six.' He had gained a general impression of the shadowy figures as they thundered past. He frowned. Something did not seem quite right; something struck him as being odd, but he could not think what it was. 'Must be imagining things,' he said to himself, but as he rode the thought kept nagging at him. 'Six!' he gasped suddenly. 'But one seemed different.' His thoughts raced. He had only got a brief look at the riders, but now he realised that something had made an impression on his mind of which he had not been aware at the time. Five of the horsemen seemed to be grouped around one, who, although the horse galloped as hard as the others, did not ride with the same zest, as if he had no will for the journey. This proved nothing as far as Bill could figure and he realised that he could have been deceived by the darkness. Bill straightened himself, kicked his horse into a gallop and was soon at the Circle C.

The following morning, as Collins rode to the Bar X, he saw Pete Young and his brother leave the ranch-house to meet him. A cursory nod was all they gave him as a greeting and they waited for him to speak first.

'Thought I'd ride over an' see if there was anythin' you wanted to know about the place,' said Collins.

'We can find our own way around,' answered Ed sharply.

Bill ignored the remark. 'One tip might be useful. I used to run the spread with ten men an' you'll need thet number when the herds trailin' north use Wayman's Ford.'

'We'll manage with the five of us,' snapped Nick. 'Now leave us to run this outfit as we like.'

'I was only tryin' to help,' replied Bill testily. 'I thought if I was to come in on this scheme of yours I would start...'

He was cut short by Ed's harsh laugh. 'Too late, Collins,' he said. 'After you'd left last night we discussed your attitude an' decided thet you weren't interested – sorry, it's too late now, we've made a start an' thet's thet. Now, if you'll excuse us, we've a lot to do.' He spun on his heel and walked away, followed by his brother.

Bill watched them for a moment before turning his horse. 'Five,' he muttered to himself. 'I'm sure there were six.'

As the clop of hoofs faded away, Ed turned to Nick. 'We'll put the pressure on straight away; he's sure to check up on our claims.'

Throughout the next ten days the Circle C suffered a number of annoying accidents; fences were broken, cattle strayed, horses were lamed, steers died and cowboys were bushwacked and beaten up. In spite of all his efforts, Bill Collins could pin the blame on no one in particular, although he had his own suspicions.

'Reports of similar incidents hev come in from all the ranches around here,' Clint told Bill one day, when Collins was in Red Springs.

'What about the Youngs?' asked Bill.

'Even they have suffered,' replied Clint. 'Seems your suspicions have been unfounded.'

Bill sighed. 'What about thet sixth rider I saw?' he said.

'Nobody else has seen him,' replied Clint. 'There are only five men out at the Bar X, reckon you've been mistaken in the dark.'

Suddenly the door of the sheriff's office burst open and Ed stormed in.

'Rustlers!' he shouted. 'Hundred head of cattle rustled and we hev a lawman here who sits around doin' nothin'!'

Clint's face darkened as he glared back at Ed. 'Hold it, Young!' he snapped. 'I can't be everywhere, besides, how was I to know your cattle was goin' to be rustled.'

'You've got nowhere with these other blows we ranchers are suffering,' snarled Ed. 'It's time our sheriff was back – thet's if he is comin' back an' if he isn't then we should hev a new lawman.'

'Now hold on,' snapped Collins, jumping

to his feet. 'You know why our sheriff isn't here. I've suffered more than any other rancher an' I ain't grumblin' at Clint. He's hardly given himself any rest tryin' to track down the lawbreakers.'

'You hevn't had cattle rustled,' rapped Ed. 'What are you goin' to do about it?' he snapped, turning to Clint.

'Guess I'll ride back with you an' take a look around, might pick up a lead,' replied Clint, pushing himself to his feet and picking up his Stetson. 'Comin' Bill?'

The three men rode at a fast pace to the Bar X, where Ed took them to the section of the range from which the cattle had been rustled. They rode around for a while, but even the experienced eyes of leather-faced Clint could not find a trail.

'Too many hoof marks to pick anythin' out,' he said. His eyes narrowed as he looked across the range. 'Reckon I'll take a ride to the south tomorrow. Only safe place to hide cattle is in the hills.'

The three men rode back to the Bar X where Clint questioned Mart Webster and Joe Burgess, who had discovered that cattle were missing. Bill Collins, who was still puzzled over the sixth man he swore he had seen, managed to slip away unnoticed. He moved swiftly around the ranch-house and stopped close to the window of what used to be his room. He peered cautiously inside, but there was no one there. He moved swiftly to the next window and was surprised to find that, not only had the blind been pulled but it was fastened to the window frame, obscuring the room completely. He stepped forward, but suddenly froze in his tracks. He tensed himself, his ear pressed close against the window. Suddenly all sight and sound was blotted out, as a Colt crashed on to the back of his head. His knees buckled, and he pitched forward to the ground.

The movement at the end of the ranch-house caught the attention of the four men who were still talking in front of the veranda.

'What the...?' gasped Ed, when he saw Wally dragging the unconscious form of Bill Collins round the corner of the building.

'Bill!' shouted Clint, leaping forward to push Wally roughly away from his old friend.

'Caught him snoopin' round the back,' said Wally, in answer to Ed's questioning look.

Ed hurried to the water trough, filled a

bucket, and threw it over Collins. The impact of the cold water stirred some life into the unconscious form. Bill's eyes flickered open, he struggled to sit up, his hands searching for the pain which throbbed in his head. Slowly his eyes focused, and with Clint's help he struggled to his feet and looked around the men about him.

'Collins,' hissed Ed, his eyes narrowed in anger, 'don't snoop around here, next time you might not be so lucky.' He turned to Clint. 'Now git him off here, an' tomorrow see thet you git some results.'

Clint glared at Ed. He was tempted to make an issue of the matter, but when he glanced at the men around him, he realised it would be useless. He helped Bill to his horse and soon the two men were riding in the direction of the Circle C.

An hour passed when the sound of hooves pounding towards the house brought Ed Brown on to the veranda. His frown vanished and a smile flicked his face when he saw four men led by Nick, riding hard.

'Howdy, boys,' greeted Ed, as they pulled to a halt. 'Make yourselves comfortable,' he added, indicating the bunk-house.

The four men wheeled their mounts and

were soon being welcomed by Mart, Wally, and Joe.

'Come on in, Nick,' said Ed, leading the way into the house. 'I see you brought men from our eastern gang.'

'Yeah,' replied his brother. 'They were the quickest and easiest to contact.'

'How do the old Wichitas look?' asked Ed.

'Fine,' replied Nick. 'It sure was good to see those old mountains again. I'll be glad when we git back there permanent.'

'It won't be long now,' said Ed. 'I've news for you. Tell you about it whilst we eat.' He crossed the room to a door which he unlocked with a key from his pocket. The window was completely covered and the only light came from a lamp which revealed a figure sobbing on the bed. 'Time for a meal, Mrs McCoy,' he called. The figure did not move. Ed stormed across the room, grabbed Barbara by the arm, jerked her off the bed and propelled her to the door. 'I said it was time for a meal,' he hissed. 'Nick's had a long ride an' he's hungry.'

Barbara stumbled against the doorpost. From the experience of the past few days she knew it was useless to protest, besides, preparing meals did enable her to get into the daylight of the kitchen. She shuffled to

129

the door, but Ed preceded her and locked the outside door of the kitchen. He grinned evilly at her as he returned to the room.

As they enjoyed the meal, Ed told Nick of the recent events. 'I'm in well with the townsfolk,' grinned Ed. 'I've let them see a lot of me, treated them to drinks, and in general let them think I'm a big shot. As fer our prominent citizens, wal, I keep putting them off with promises and tellin' them we must git settled in here first an' git this trouble cleared up. But I've got them so keen they'll back me in anythin'.'

Nick laughed. 'Good work Ed, but when do we really git to work?'

'Tonight,' announced Ed. 'You couldn't hev returned at a better time. I've faked this rustlin' here so folks will think we are in the clear. I've been lettin' off steam around town about the inefficiency of Clint Schofield an' now this rustlin' will put him worse off. After tonight we can really git him kicked out.'

'What's on tonight?' asked Nick eagerly, as Ed paused to light a cheroot.

'Collins has about sixty valuable horses corralled at the Circle C, ready to sell to Jeb Bond, a rancher about fifty miles from here. The shipment is due to take place tomorrow, so I figure if we git those horses tonight

130

Collins will suffer his first severe blow, an' we'll be able to throw further inefficiency at Schofield.'

Nick grinned. 'This is somethin' like,' he said eagerly, and the two men discussed the forthcoming raid after which they went over it again with the rest of their men.

Darkness had already cast its blanket over the Texas countryside when Nick Brown led the four newcomers towards the Circle C. Mart Webster and Joe Burgess had accompanied them to within a mile of the ranch, when they had headed to a position in a small hollow which ran south from the ranch-house. They were to wait there and help to run the horses south. Ed and Wally remained at the Bar X.

When the buildings of the Circle C appeared as a dark mass ahead Nick called a halt, slipped from his saddle and ordered the men to await his return. Silently he vanished into the darkness and reappeared just as silently as few minutes later, after reconnoitering the ranch.

'Bill Collins is in bed, reckon he don't feel so good after Wally dealt with him today,' he said. 'His cowpokes are all in the bunkhouse. The horses are in two corrals on this

131

side of the house. Two of you will take one corral, two of you the other. I'll fire the bunk-house, an' in the confusion we should be able to drive those horses southwards along the hollow to where Mart and Joe will be waitin' to lend a hand. They know where to take them. I'll be returning to the Bar X when I see everythin' has gone right.'

As there were no questions, Nick led the way stealthily forward. They reached the corrals without mishap and the four men took up their positions ready to release the horses at Nick's prearranged signal.

Nick hurried forward and on reaching the back of the hut, he lit the ready-made torch and applied it to the dry timber of the wall. Flames licked hungrily at the wood and when Nick was satisfied it was well alight, he threw the remains of the torch on to the roof.

As soon as the men at the corrals saw it fly through the air they opened the corral gates and, shouting and yelling, drove the horses out. Two of them positioned themselves quickly alongside the stampeding animals, funelling them along the narrow hollow, whilst the other two prepared to ride in behind. Nick had reached his horse, but instead of mounting, drew his Colt and turned to face the burning building. Shouts and yells indicated the Circle C cowboys were running from the bunk-house. As two of them appeared round the building, calling to the others to get after the horses, Nick loosed off two shots from his Colt. One man stopped in his tracks and pitched forward to the ground. The other grasped his shoulder and leaped for cover. A third man appeared round the other end of the bunk-house and fired in Nick's direction, but as the bullet whistled harmlessly past, Nick turned sharply and dropped the man into a silent heap before he had time to fire again. Seeing that all the horses were out of the corrals and his men were pounding away from the Circle C, Nick leaped into the saddle and sent his horse into a fast gallop along the hollow. When he was satisfied that all was going well, he swung away in the direction of the Bar X.

Bill Collins came out of a deep sleep. He still felt shaky from the blow on the head and as he stirred his brain was pounding. Suddenly, he realised that the pounding came from the door. He sat up and as his eyes cleared he was aware of a flickering light which lit the room from the outside.

He leaped from the bed and flung open the door, to find a wide-eyed agitated foreman confronting him.

'Bunk-house on fire; horses gone!'

Collins gasped, grabbed his trousers, pushed his feet into his boots and ran from the house.

He stared in horror at the empty corrals and the blaze which his men were endeavouring to control with a water chain.

'How many of them?' he asked.

'Don't know,' replied the foreman. 'With the fire taking our attention we didn't see them an' the horses were out of the corrals before we realised it. Two of the boys were killed an' one wounded when we headed fer the corrals.'

'Which way did they go?'

'Up the hollow, Mister Collins. Here's Zeke with three horses.'

Even as Collins and his foreman leaped into the saddle and lashed the animals into an earth-pounding gallop, he knew pursuit would be useless; the rustlers had too much start. After about three miles' hard riding Collins called a halt.

'It's no use,' he said dejectedly. 'We'll try again in the mornin', but I doubt if we'll find a lead.'

They turned their horses and rode back to the ranch, where they found the weary ranch-hands miserably watching the smouldering ruins of their bunk-house.

Collins had just slipped from the saddle when the pound of hooves startled him and two figures emerged from the darkness.

Ed and Nick pulled their horses to a halt in front of Bill.

'Saw the glow from the Bar X,' said Ed. 'Thought you might need help. Seems we're a bit late,' he added, indicating the smoking ruin.

Collins eyed him disdainfully. 'Hundred head of horses rustled as well as two men dead.'

Ed whistled. 'My cattle, and now your horses. These hombres are sure strikin' fast an' hard. Hev any luck?' he asked, indicating Bill's horse.

Collins shook his head. 'I'm sendin' word to Schofield so he...'

'Useless,' interrupted Nick. 'A lot of people around here are not satisfied with the way he's tackled things lately. If he doesn't turn somethin' up tomorrow, there'll be trouble!'

Clint Schofield rode slowly into Red Springs. He felt weary and dejected. He knew people

135

were saying he had not handled the troubles correctly, and with two rustlings, one quickly upon the other, various ranchers were concerned and getting angry. Matters were not helped any by the fact that the Youngs, in their subtle way, seemed to be agitating the people against him.

The news of the raid on the Circle C, had come as a shock to him, but he felt confident that the rustlers must be operating from the hills to the south and, knowing the country as well as anybody, he had persuaded the men who wanted to ride with him to stay behind, saying that one man would be less likely to raise the suspicions of the rustlers.

Now, Clint returned after a fruitless search and knew the trouble which awaited him. By the time he reached his office a crowd had gathered, and as he slipped from the saddle and hitched his horse to the rail, he noticed that Pete Young, accompanied by a stranger, pushed his way to the front of the crowd.

'What happened, Schofield?' someone shouted.

Clint stepped on to the sidewalk and turned slowly to face the crowd.

'Not a sign,' he answered.

136

Bill Collins moved forward, his face showing that he could hardly believe Clint's words. 'Nothin' at all, Clint?' he said.

The deputy sheriff shook his head. 'I've searched everywhere I thought possible.'

Young, putting on the act of an angry man, jumped on to the sidewalk. 'We've all been waitin' here fer nothin'. We expected to be ridin' now to round up the rustlers. We should hev all gone in the first place, but you thought otherwise.'

A murmur ran through the crowd.

'Thet wouldn't hev been much good either,' answered Clint, a new fire blazing in his eyes, as he saw accusations in Young's words.

'You hevn't done much good since all this trouble started,' shouted Ed.

'An' we didn't hev trouble until your outfit came here!' Clint answered, glaring angrily at Ed.

'Accusin' me of heving somethin' to do with it?' snapped Ed. 'I've lost cattle, remember? You've nothin' to lose; could be you were coverin' up; you were keen to go alone!'

Clint stiffened as the words stung him. The murmurings of the crowd grew louder and sensing he had made an impact, Ed

137

seized the opportunity.

'Only Collins an' I hev been raided on a large scale, but whose turn will it be next?' he yelled. 'How much protection will you get from Schofield?'

Stung by the implication of the words the crowd grew restless. Angry shouts were hurled at Clint.

'Hold it, hold it!' shouted Collins, raising his arms. 'Clint's served this town well, he wouldn't...'

'How do you know?' shouted Ed. 'There's always a first time! I say we do somethin' about it.'

'Like what?' snapped Clint.

'Like gettin' someone else as sheriff,' replied Ed.

A roar of approval greeted this proposal.

'You can't do thet,' yelled Collins. 'Dan McCoy's sheriff of this town.'

'An' where is he?' snapped backed Ed. 'He should be here lookin' after the interests of the folks.'

Shouts of agreement came from all sides.

'You all know where he is,' shouted Clint. 'Anyone would hev done the same if your wife had been kidnapped.'

The tone of the crowd eased a little, but Ed roused them again.

'An' whilst we wait fer his return we are goin' to suffer at the hands of an incompetent deputy,' he shouted. 'How do we know he isn't dead? Let's have a new sheriff!'

The crowed roared its approval. Clint tensed himself and suddenly made a move for his gun.

'I wouldn't if I was you!' a voice rapped, and Clint found himself staring into the cold muzzle of a Colt in the hands of the stranger. Clint's hand moved away from his holster.'

'Thanks,' said Ed to the stranger, and turned to Clint.

'That was foolish, Schofield,' he said. 'If the people of this town want a new sheriff, they shall hev one an' you won't stop them with a gun.'

The crowd yelled support for Ed.

Shoving his Colt back into its holster, the stranger stepped on to the sidewalk. 'I was jest passin' through, as some of you know from our acquaintance in the saloon. Seems I've run into local trouble, but if I can be of any help, I'll take the job on until your own man comes back or you appoint someone else. My name's Mike Yates an' I was once a sheriff up in Wyoming.'

Ed grinned. 'Wall, here's the very man,' he

shouted. 'I'm willin' to accept his proposition. Anyone else do the same?'

Shouts of agreement grew louder.

'Then it's settled,' said Mike. 'Sorry, Schofield, but the folks want it thet way. I'll expect you out of the office in an hour.'

Clint glared angrily at him. Hot words leaped to his lips, but he left them unspoken, spun on his heel, and hurried into his office.

The crowd split up and Ed and Mike walked across to the saloon. Bill Collins watched them for a moment, then followed Clint into the office.

'I'm sorry, Clint,' he said.

The weather-beaten face was dark with anger. 'It's not your fault,' replied Clint. 'There's something' wrong here an' I'll bet Pete Young's at the bottom of it. Convenient thet hombre was in town, an' I'll guess Pete Young knows him. He wants me out of the way fer some reason.'

'Come back to the Circle C with me,' invited Bill. 'Work on your own from there.'

'It's my guess things will quieten down fer a while,' said Clint, 'so thet everyone thinks this hombre is doin' his job.' He paused thoughtfully. 'Young has a sheriff on his side, an' thet could lead to bigger things and an eventual take-over of the town by the Youngs.'

'Could be you're right,' said Bill. 'I don't know. I'm all confused with Barbara's disappearance, the take-over of the Bar X, an' then losin' all those horses. What are you goin' to do, Clint?'

'Reckon if you'll keep your eyes open at this end, Bill, I'll ride north an' try to contact Dan an' let him know what's happenin' in Red Springs.'

Chapter Ten

Unaware of the events in Red Springs, Dan and the Collins brothers awaited news of the Browns.

A week went by without a word, and Dan was becoming more and more uneasy. One evening he went to the saloon and sought out Curt Jackson.

'Curt,' he said. 'We're gettin' fed up of hangin' around; do the Browns always work as slow as this?'

'No one questions the way the Browns work,' snapped Curt.

'Wal, I do,' rapped back Dan. 'Way back in...'

'They're the bosses,' cut in Jackson viciously, 'an' we work their way, slow or fast.' His tone eased. 'They do all right by us all – plenty of cash, an' here you hev wine, women, an' song, so what more do you want?'

'Action!' snapped Dan. 'We're three men thet like action. If it's always goin' to be as slow as this, then I guess we'll move on.'

Curt straightened from the bar, his eyes cold with anger, his voice low but sharp with meaning. 'Once in the Browns' gang, you never leave, unless it's with a bullet in you.'

Dan smiled. 'It's my hunch the Browns hev left the Wichitas; left us all without a word.' He saw Curt stiffen and he hoped that if the outlaw knew the whereabouts of his leaders, he would let it slip in a quick answer, but Curt did not speak. Puzzled, Dan pressed the matter. 'If they've gone, let's operate by ourselves. I'd hev more raids an'...'

'Fergit it, Ferguson,' cut in Jackson. 'The Browns hev never let us down; if they've left the mountains, it will be to git information regarding another raid. Small raids an' often is out; big raids, less frequently are better, because there's less chance of gettin' caught.'

'Wal, when are we likely to hear from them?' snapped Dan.

'I've told you, I don't know,' answered Jackson. 'Could be a few days, or a few weeks.'

'Then don't be surprised if we lose patience an' go,' warned Dan.

Curt's eyes narrowed. 'Try to run out,' he hissed, 'an' it'll be the last thing you do.'

Dan glared at him, but without another word he spun on his heel and left the saloon. Back at the hotel he sought out Jack and Howard and told them of his interview with Jackson.

'I tried to draw him,' he said, 'but I've come to the conclusion that he really doesn't know anythin'.'

'Then it looks as if we'll jest hev to sit tight an' await events,' said Jack.

'I've an uneasy feelin' thet somethin's gone amiss,' said Dan, 'an' thet the Browns hev left. I'm goin' scoutin' in the mountains to see if I can pick up any trace of them.'

'We'll take the area in sections an' search one each,' suggested Howard.

Dan shook his head. 'If three of us ride out together, Jackson will think we're runnin' out on the gang, but if you two stay he won't be suspicious.'

When Dan returned to Lone Wolf after four days in the Wichita Mountains, the Collins brothers greeted him eagerly when he entered the hotel, but their hopeful anticipation of success vanished when they saw the hopelessness registered on Dan's face.

He sat down wearily. 'Not a sign,' he muttered. 'They could have disappeared off the face of the earth for all I found. It's hopeless. We'll never see Barbara again.'

Although he felt disappointed, Jack realised he must do something to rouse Dan out of his despondency. 'It's not hopeless,' he snapped. 'You can't hev searched all the mountains in four days.'

'I know,' replied Dan. 'But I came across no sign whatsoever. They must have left the mountains.'

'Wal, suppose they have,' said Jack. 'It will only be fer a while. They're not goin' to leave this set-up in the Wichitas. They'll be back, an' like Curt said they'll contact him. All we hev to do is to sit tight, an' wait.'

'Wait!' snapped Dan, pounding the bed with his fist. 'Wait! An' all the time Barbara's in danger.' His face was grim; his eyes narowed. 'If they've harmed one hair of her head, I'll gun them down, same as I killed their brothers,' he hissed.

His threat still hung on the air as the door crashed open. The three men, their hands flying towards their holsters, spun to face the door.

'Leave them!' snapped Curt Jackson as he entered the room, the cold muzzle of a Colt covering the Texans. He glared angrily at the three men. 'Lawmen,' he hissed. 'I might hev known it. I always thought there was somethin' strange about you right from the start, and yet you did well. I can't figure you out. Thought you'd been up to somethin' when you were missin' fer four days. Jest as well I saw you ride in an' followed you up here. Now things tie up a bit better. But who's this Barbara?'

'My wife,' replied Dan. 'Brown's kidnapped her.'

Curt grinned. 'Heard about a tin star in Texas thet hed killed two of their brothers. Guess they were smart gettin' your wife. You were bound to come lookin'. Wal, they'll be mighty pleased when they hear I killed the three of you.'

Dan stiffened. He knew Jackson would be ruthless.

'You can't shoot the three of us, Curt,' said Dan quietly. 'You may git one or two, but as soon as you start squeezin' thet trigger we'll be reachin' fer our guns; one of us will git you.'

Curt grinned. 'You're right, but I don't intend to shoot you here. I could git you to unfasten your gun belts, but I figure you might even pull somethin' then, so I'm goin' to march you out of here an' enlist the aid of some of the boys. Now, raise your arms an' git movin'.'

Dan realised that desperate situations required desperate measures. He was standing beside a table on which there was a cup of water and as he began to raise his arms, he swept up the cup and in one swift movement, threw it at the outlaw. At the same time, estimating that the first bullet would be meant for him, he flung himself to one side, crashing into Howard. The two men stumbled and as they did so, the roar of a Colt filled the room, but, as Curt had automatically ducked, his aim was off target and the bullet crashed harmlessly into the wall.

In the same split second a Colt had leaped to Jack's hand and the bullet found its mark, crashing into Jackson's shoulder, sending him reeling against the doorpost. In vain he tried to raise his arm to fire again, but a second bullet pounded into his chest. His eyes widened in a glassy stare, and he slid to the floor in a crumpled heap.

Dan and the Collins brothers leaped through the door and hurled themselves down the stairs, two at a time. The startled proprietor jumped out of the way as, with guns in hand, they ran across the lobby and on to the sidewalk, where they sized up the situation in one swift glance. Men were already running towards the hotel and as the three friends burst out of the door, guns were dragged from holsters, but before a shot could be fired in their direction, Dan and the Collins brothers scattered the approaching men with a fusillade of shots.

Seizing the moment's respite when the men dived for cover, they leaped for their horses, flung themselves into the saddles and turned their mounts into a fast gallop as bullets began to fly in their direction. The three men flattened themselves along the horses' backs, calling to the animals for greater speed. As they hurtled towards the edge of town Dan glanced at Howard and was startled to see a damp, red patch staining the sleeve of Howard's shirt! Glancing over his shoulder, he saw that several men were already in the saddle, pounding in pursuit.

Earth flew as flashing hoofs thundered along the trail and after a mile Dan saw that blood still oozed from Howard's arm. He realised that Howard would not be able to keep up a desperate flight for a long time. Somehow they must shake off their pursuers.

Dan glanced behind him and his eyes widened with surprise.

'We've lost four of them!' he shouted,

148

hardly able to believe that there were only five riders behind them.

In eager anticipation at out-riding the remaining five riders, the three men urged their horses to greater effort. Somehow, the strong animals stretched themselves in answer and the gap widened.

Half a mile further on, found them nearing the spot where Dan had been shot some days previously. As they rounded a bend in the trail, they suddenly hauled hard on the reins, bringing their horses to a long, sliding, earth-tearing halt. A short distance ahead, four men were dropping on to the trail from the steep hillside! Dan cursed himself for not realising that these men knew the mountains and had taken a short cut to head them off. He looked round desperately; to their left was a steep hillside, impossible to climb at this point, to their right was a steep incline to a river below.

Already the four men were drawing their guns and moving towards them, and round the bend the pound of hoofs was growing louder.

'Down to the river,' yelled Dan, realising it was better to risk the slope than be caught in a cross-fire. He leaped from his saddle and threw the reins to Jack. 'We'll be easy targets on that slope,' he shouted. 'I'll hold them off until you reach the water.'

Jack started to protest. 'But you…'

'I'll be all right,' cut in Dan. He pulled his rifle from its leather and hurried to the cover of a boulder.

Although reluctant to leave Dan, the brothers knew he was right and put their horses at the slope. Jack's horse hesitated, but he urged it forward and the unwilling animal went over the edge. As it moved Jack felt a bullet whine close to his head. The next moment he was slithering and sliding with the two animals, in the wake of Howard, who was already sending stones and earth rolling towards the river.

Dan watched the four men carefully as they approached cautiously along the trail. Suddenly, one loosed off a bullet just before Jack headed down the slope. Dan replied with his rifle and saw the man spin round and fall. The other three quickly sought the protection of some rocks and started firing rapidly in Dan's direction. Dan held his fire, keeping careful watch from behind his boulder. Suddenly, the firing ceased; Dan eased his rifle, and when he saw one of the outlaws, curious because there was no answering fire, peer out from behind the rock, he squeezed the trigger. A shout died in the man's throat and he pitched forward on to the trail.

The pound of hoofs brought Dan's attention to the other five pursuers. He turned his rifle towards the bend in the trail and as the riders hurtled round the corner he fired rapidly. Surprised by the greeting, the outlaws hauled hard on the reins, pulled the animals round and drove them away from the whining bullets. Dan saw one man jerk in the saddle and as the frightened horse reared, he crashed to the ground and lay still.

Once they were round the corner, the outlaws flung themselves from the saddles and dropped behind protective rocks, from which they opened fire at Dan. Lead flew thick and fast from both sides, forcing Dan to crouch low behind the boulder. He glanced anxiously down the slope and was relieved to see that Jack and Howard had almost reached the river. He knew that unless he acted quickly he would not escape. This withering fire could keep him pinned down, whilst some of the outlaws worked their way into more advantageous positions from which they would have sight of an unprotected Dan.

He saw Jack and Howard reach the bottom

151

of the slope safely, and force the animals into the water. Taking advantage of a slight respite in the shooting, Dan jumped to his feet and loosed off a couple of shots as he leaped towards the edge of the slope. Bullets whistled around him as he flung himself over the edge. His breath was almost driven from his body when he hit the ground, but relaxing quickly, he rolled over and over, bringing stones and earth tumbling after him as he hurtled faster down the steep slope towards the river. He shot off the bottom of the incline and plunged down into the water, the coldness of which shocked him back into reality. He struck upwards and broke the surface gasping for breath. He looked round quickly and swam after the two brothers who were making good progress towards the opposite bank. Dan glanced over his shoulder and saw that the outlaws were already lined along the top of the slope. Bullets were flung after him, more in desperation than in accuracy, but knowing that a chance bullet could be deadly, Dan kept up his strong stroke until he was half way across the river and out of range of the outlaws' guns. Only then did he relax for a moment, and look behind. He saw the outlaws were coaxing their horses and carefully picking their way down the steep slope to the river. Dan struck out for the river bank where Jack and Howard were already urging their mounts on to dry land. Eager hands pulled Dan from the water and once on shore they quickly reviewed the situation.

Howard's arm had suffered only a flesh wound and once they had stemmed the flow of blood, and secured the horses at a safe distance from the river, they returned to the bank with the rifles and guns which the Collins brothers had kept dry. They immediately opened fire on the outlaws in the water and two men toppled from their horses' backs. The others returned the fire but, realising that seated on swimming horses they were easy targets for the men on the bank, they turned their horses and headed back for the opposite bank. Dan and the brothers sent a parting volley after them and watched the men reach the bank, where they held a brief conference before taking their horses up the hill and riding off in the direction of Lone Wolf.

'Reckon we've shaken thet lot off,' grinned Dan, as he climbed to his feet.

'But what about Barbara?' asked Jack. 'We can't contact the Browns through their gang now.'

The smile disappeared from Dan's face; he looked grim as he tackled the problem. 'There's something thet doesn't ring right to me,' he said. 'I still hev a feelin' they've left the mountains. I reckon we'll play my hand, leave the Wichitas an' see if we can pick up a clue at some town or ranch; a lone girl with a gang of men would be sure to attract attention.'

The three men made their way through the mountains to the town of Apache, where the sheriff, Bill Dawson, was pleased to see them again, and was most interested to hear their story.

'Wal, sheriff,' Dan concluded, 'I figure if we leave our share of the bank robbery with you you'll see it gits back to Texola.'

'Shore,' replied Dawson. 'They'll be mighty glad to see some of it back. Heard about thet raid; it shook the whole territory. No one could figure how the robbers had disappeared so quickly. Now we know thet what's left of them are in Lone Wolf. I'll organise a posse, gun them out, an' recover the money.'

'Good,' said Dan, 'thet'll ease our consciences over our part in the raid. When we catch up with the Browns, we hope we might recover most of the remainder.'

'Thanks,' answered Dawson. 'I'm sorry I hev no news of the Browns. I've had no report on them since the news of the raid in Texola.'

'Wal, I guess we'll drift southwards,' said Dan. 'Thanks fer your help.'

'Sorry I couldn't do more,' replied Dawson. 'Best of luck.'

The three men from Red Springs left Apache via the south road. For two days they rode southwards, through the territory, enquiring of anyone and everyone as to whether a posse of horsemen accompanied by a young woman had been seen.

It was dark on the second day's ride from Apache when they rode wearily into a dusty, one-street town.

'Reckon we might as well hev a bed tonight,' said Dan as they pulled up outside the wooden-fronted hotel.

After they had booked their rooms, bathed and had a good, solid meal, they wandered to the saloon.

'Our only chance here is drifters,' said Howard, pushing open the batwings. 'The Browns wouldn't venture into town.'

'Only to buy supplies, an' then only one or two men would come in to do it,' said Jack. 'We'll check at the store tomorrow and see if

155

anyone's bought any large supplies recently.'

Reaching the bar they called for three beers and whilst they enjoyed them, they surveyed the saloon.

'Look like local men,' observed Howard.

'Yeah,' agreed Jack. 'But some of them may hev been out of town an' seen some- thin',' he added hopefully.

Dan finished his beer and was about to move away from the bar, when Howard stopped him and nodded towards the bat- wings.

They swung behind a small, dust-covered man whom Dan reckoned to be in his sixties. His clothes were worn and his hat battered and dirty, but he walked towards the bar with a determined step.

Dan called for four beers. 'Reckon you look as if you could do with one,' he said, turning towards the old man as he reached the bar. 'Wash some of the dust out of your throat.'

The old man looked Dan up and down and liked what he saw. 'Thet's mighty nice of you, young fella,' he grinned. 'I've hed a long, hard trip an' haven't seen the inside of a glass fer a month.' He drank eagerly and Dan ordered another, as he watched the man enjoy the drink. He saw a weather-beaten, wrinkled face which had a friendliness reflected in the eyes.

'Been prospectin'?' asked Dan.

The old man wiped the beer from his moustache before he spoke. 'Yeah,' he replied.

'Any luck,' queried Dan.

'A little,' grinned the prospector. 'Haven't made a fortune, but what I found'll help me along a bit.'

'Good,' said Dan. 'You haven't by any chance seen any riders – maybe three or four men an' a girl of about twenty-five with them?'

The man looked at Dan curiously. 'Matter of fact I hev,' he said casually.

'What!' Dan gasped, his eyes widening with surprise at the news. He looked eagerly at Jack and Howard, who were equally taken aback at suddenly hearing news they had almost given up hope of hearing.

'Where?' said Dan eagerly.

'I was down near the Red River about a week back; saw this girl ridin' as if the devil were after her. Then they appeared; five of them. She didn't hev a chance to escape; cut her off, but she was a game 'un; plunged into the river. It wasn't any use; if they hedn't pulled her out the river would hev

157

got her.' He paused to sip his beer.

'What happened to them?' asked Jack anxiously.

'Can't rightly say,' replied the old man. 'They started a fire, looking as if they might be making camp. I thought of ridin' in to see what it was all about, but then I figured it was none of my business, besides, five to one, wal those are odds even I'm doubtful of takin' on.'

Dan grinned. 'You did right, old timer, but you've shore helped us.'

'Know them?' asked the prospector curiously.

'Yeah,' replied Dan. 'Two of them are the Brown brothers who operate in the Wichitas. Kidnapped my wife from Red Springs some time back; I've been after them ever since.'

'Then you'll be Dan McCoy,' said the old man excitedly.

Dan and the Collins brothers stared at him incredulously. 'How do you know my name?' gasped Dan.

'Ran across an old friend of mine yesterday, ain't seen him for twenty years,' he explained. 'Name of Clint Schofield.'

'Clint!' gasped Dan. 'What's he doin' up here?'

'Lookin' fer you,' answered the prospector. 'Told me all your trouble an' there's more besides, thet you don't know about.'

Dan looked sharply at Jack and Howard. A frown creased his forehead. 'What you mean?' he asked. 'Where was Clint headin'?'

'North,' grinned the old man, 'but if you'll git yourself over to the hotel, you'll find him bookin' rooms fer us both. As I hedn't had a beer fer a month he sent me in here whilst he went to git us fixed up. Guess he'll be here any minute.'

'C'm on, we'll go an' see him,' said Dan, but before they could move from the bar, the batwings creaked open. The four men spun round to see who had entered the saloon.

'Clint!' yelled Dan and the Collins brothers together, leaping forward to greet their friend.

Clint gasped. He gripped them eagerly by the hand, but was so surprised that it was a few moments before he could speak.

Ten minutes later, Clint had finished telling them of the troubles in Red Springs, and was faced by three worried men.

'We've got to get back now,' said Dan. 'You boys should be with our father an' I...'

'But we've just got a lead on Barbara,' cut in Jack. 'You follow it up Dan, Howard and

I will…'

'I can't,' interrupted Dan. 'I was put in as Sheriff of Red Springs; I owe a duty to the people of the town. These hombres are trying to take things over; I should be there.'

'But what about Barbara?' protested Howard.

'There's no one wants to follow up this lead more than I do,' pointed out Dan, 'but thet trail could be cold by now. It's back to Red Springs an' then we can try an' pick up the trail of the Browns after things are cleared up in Red Springs.'

The brothers knew it was useless to protest any further now that Dan had his mind made up and early the next morning four grim-faced men headed for the Texas border.

Chapter Eleven

'Wal, Collins, thet's my offer, take or leave it; but I'm warning you, don't expect it to be so high if there's less cattle to buy, or any more buildings hev been damaged.' Ed Brown looked hard at the man seated dejectedly at the table.

Bill Collins stared at the man he knew as Pete Young.

'I can't understand it,' he muttered hoarsely. 'Why me? Why hev I been picked out by this gang which is ridin' the territory?'

'You aren't the only one thet's been hit,' pointed out Ed. 'We've suffered at the Bar X, an' other ranchers hev hed cattle rustled.'

'Shore they hev,' agreed Collins, 'but no one's been hit as hard as I hev, stampedes, rustlin', buildings burnt, an' cowboys terrorised until I've only two left apart from my foreman an' myself. What's this new sheriff done about it?'

'Now be fair, Collins,' came the reply. 'You know thet he's broken up several raids in the district, one of them on this ranch, but he

161

can't succeed every time. At least he's been more successful than Schofield.'

Bill Collins nodded. He had to admit that what Pete said was true, but if only he could have read the thoughts behind the smoke, he would have realised how cleverly everything had been engineered; the raids planned carefully so that no suspicion would fall on the Youngs, and the sheriff tipped off so that it would appear he was defeating the rustlers.

Bill looked up at Pete. 'Your offer is a tempting one, Young,' he said, rubbing his chin thoughtfully. 'All this comin' on top of the fact that you claimed the Bar X, has brought me to the point of ruin.'

'I thought you were in a pretty bad way thet's why I'm makin' this offer,' replied Ed.

'If the rustlers are determined to ruin the Circle C they won't stop even if you take over,' pointed out Collins.

'I've thought of thet,' answered Ed. 'With the Circle C and the Bar X to run, I'll need a lot more men, an' therefore I reckon I'll be a match fer the rustlers.' He paused to let his words sink in. 'What do you say to selling?'

Bill shook his head sadly. 'I don't know,' he muttered. 'If only Jack an' Howard hed been here.' He stared at the table with unseeing eyes for a few moments, turning the problem over in his mind. Suddenly, a decision made, he looked up.

'No,' he rapped. 'I'll not sell, I'll fight to the end!'

Ed shrugged his shoulders. 'As you will,' he replied. 'I admire a man who'll fight for what is his.'

'Thanks fer your offer, all the same,' said Bill, rising to his feet. 'It would hev been an easy way out, but I was never one to back out of a fight.'

Ed rode back to the Bar X and grinned as he entered the ranch-house. His brother Nick looked up from the chair in which he sprawled, enjoying a glass of whisky.

'Somethin' pleasin' you, Ed?' drawled Nick.

'I've jest been visitin' Bill Collins,' he replied, helping himself to a drink. 'Offered to help him out by buyin' his spread.'

'What!' Nick jerked upright in his chair. 'Thet was a crazy thing to do when we're goin' to git it fer nothin'.'

Ed smiled. 'Not so crazy as you think. I didn't expect him to sell – he's a determined old fool – but my offer put us in good standing with him an' he's less likely to suspect us.'

Nick grinned and relaxed. 'Smart work, Ed. When are we goin' to finish off the job?'

'Tonight, I reckon,' answered Ed. 'As soon as it's dark. There's only Collins, his foreman an' two men left, so we'll fire the house.'

Nick drained his glass. 'An' thet'll finish off Collins. With Schofield run out of his job an' McCoy killed by Joe back in the Wichitas, we're in possession of these two spreads and our revenge is complete.'

Ed nodded. 'There's only one thing I regret,' he said quietly, thet I didn't git my gun on McCoy.'

Darkness was gathering across the Texas countryside when the Browns, accompanied by Joe Burgess and three other men, rode steadily away from the Bar X towards the Circle C. It was dark by the time they pulled to a halt a short distance from the house. They secured their horses and crept silently forward, moving cautiously in case Collins had posted a guard, but they saw no one. Close to the house they halted and when Ed gave the signal the three men hurried forward, lit the prepared torches and, breaking the windows of the rooms where there were no lights, they threw them inside. Two further torches were lit quickly and thrown

164

on to the roof. The fire took hold quickly and as the three men ran swiftly to their horses the flames leaped upwards with a devouring roar. The door of the ranch-house burst open and four startled men, with guns in hands, ran out. Seeing three men pushing their horses away at a fast gallop they loosed off some shots, but the riders were too far away for the aim to be effective.

Ed grinned when he saw them turn and stare hopelessly at the house, which was now a mass of flames. He nodded to his two companions. They raised their rifles slowly, and, as the sights covered three of the men near the house, they squeezed the triggers. The two Circle C cowboys spun round and buckled into silent heaps. As Bill Collins fell, his foreman caught him and before another shot could be fired, he had pulled him behind the protection of the burning house.

'An' thet's the end of Collins,' grinned Ed. 'C'm on, let's go.'

The three men hurried to their horses and rode away from the Circle C until they reached the darkness beyond the edge of the light thrown by the leaping flames, when Nick Brown called a halt.

'I reckon we should wait here a while,' he said. 'I'm not so sure we killed Collins, thet foreman dragged him away.'

'Automatic reaction to do thet,' replied Ed. 'But it might be fun to watch the place burn right down.'

The three men turned their horses and sat silently but jubilantly, watching the inferno. They could see the foreman kneeling beside a figure on the ground. He raised Collins' head, and gave him a drink.

'Can't be dead,' said Nick. 'Reckon I'll slip back there an' finish them both off.' He pulled his rifle from its leather and was about to swing from the saddle when Ed stopped him. Above the roar of the flames, they could hear the pound of hoofs.

Four men galloped out of the darkness and brought their horses to a sliding halt.

'Clint Schofield!' hissed Nick.

Joe Burgess, his eyes widening with amazement, stiffened in the saddle, but before he could speak Ed Brown gasped.

'Ferguson! The Alvastons!'

'What the hell are they doin' here with Schofield?' snapped Nick.

Burgess stared at the two men. 'Ferguson? Alvaston? What are you talkin' about?' he said. 'Thet's Dan McCoy, an' the other two are the Collins brothers!'

'What!' Ed and Nick looked incredulously

at Burgess. 'Can't be,' went on Ed. 'They rode with us at Texola!'

'What!' It was Joe's turn to be surprised. The three men stared at each other.

'I told you McCoy was smart.' Joe Burgess broke the silence. 'He got on the inside with Curt Jackson's set-up, hopin' to get a line on you an' find his wife.'

'Thought you said you'd killed him,' snapped Nick.

'I thought I had,' replied Joe, 'but I tell you, this hombre…'

'Never mind,' interrupted Ed. 'Don't know how he knew we'd left the Wichitas, but he's here now an' we still hold the trump card.' He paused thoughtfully. 'Maybe he doesn't know we're here – Schofield doesn't know who we really are, an' McCoy may hev returned because there's been trouble in Red Springs.'

'Let's git him now,' urged Nick.

'Too risky. They're too much on the alert,' answered Ed, indicating the group of men. 'Let's git back to the Bar X.'

The three men turned their horses and rode in silence to the ranch.

'You'd better come in, Joe,' said Ed Brown, as they pulled up outside the ranch-house. 'I hev somethin' in mind an' I might need your help.'

The three men went inside and when the lamp was lit and drinks poured out, Ed turned to Burgess.

'Joe,' he said, 'do you know any good hide-outs around here?'

Joe looked thoughtful.

'What fer?' asked Nick curiously.

'We're sure to git a visit from McCoy,' explained Ed, 'an' I figure it would be better if we took his wife away from here. I aim we should disappear fer a while.'

'Won't it look strange if we aren't around?' queried Nick.

'No,' answered Ed. 'We'll leave Mart in charge, an' he can say we've gone south, cattle buyin'.'

'I reckon we should face them an' hev it out,' said Nick. 'You aren't gettin' scared, are you?' he added scornfully.

Ed stiffened. 'You know me,' he snapped. 'I jest want to see McCoy squirm a bit longer.'

'Don't overdo it,' warned Burgess. 'I know this McCoy. He's hot stuff.'

'There's always someone better, an' you're lookin' right at him,' boasted Ed. 'Now, do you know a hide-out?'

'Shore,' replied Joe. 'I found it when I was down here with the Pickerings. About half a mile before the rapids down on the Brazos. There's a cutting runs back from the river into the scrub an' thorn country in which you've got the rustled horses an' cattle hidden. You can only reach it from the river.'

'What about from the range?' asked Nick.

'The scrub an' thorns are too thick; you helped clear a way in fer the cattle, you should know what it's like. I've never known anyone to go through there.'

'Wal, how do you reach it?' asked Nick. 'The bank is too steep to walk along.'

'There's a narrow shelf under the water alongside the bank,' explained Joe. 'It runs as far as the cutting and the river just comes up to the knees. You've got to be careful or you'll be into the river an' the rapids are not far away.'

'Anyone else know about it?' asked Ed.

'Not thet I know of,' replied Joe. 'I never saw anyone go there nor heard anyone talk about it, but I can't tell what's happened since I was last down here.'

'Sounds the ideal spot,' said Ed enthusiastically. 'Dawn tomorrow you can take us there.'

Joe nodded, drained his glass, and left to get some rest.

Darkness was gathering over the Texas countryside as Dan, Clint and the Collins brothers neared Red Springs.

'We'll give the town the slip an' ride straight out to see your pa,' suggested Dan.

There was silent assent and the four men rode on grimly, wondering what they would find when they reached the Circle C. They were about two miles from the ranch when suddenly the darkness ahead was split by a light which flared into a flame and a moment later shot skywards in a devouring fire. Without a word the four men lashed their horses into a fast gallop.

'It's the house!' yelled Jack, as they neared the ranch and a few minutes later they burst out of the darkness into the eerie, flickering pool of light.

The foreman, kneeling beside Bill Collins, spun round, reaching for his gun, but, recognising Clint Schofield, left the weapon in its holster. His eyes took in the other riders as they hauled their mounts to a sliding halt and he gasped with surprise when he recognised Jack, Howard and Dan.

They were out of the saddles and beside him almost before their horses had stopped.

'Pa!' yelled Jack, when he saw his father on the ground.

'What happened?' asked Howard anxiously.

'He'll be all right,' reassured the foreman. 'Bullet grazed his head, knocked him out more than anythin' else.'

'Who did it?' asked Dan.

The foreman shook his head. 'Don't know,' he replied. 'Wish we did, then we'd know who's been causin' all the trouble around here.'

Dan looked out into the darkness. 'Reckon they're still out there?' he queried.

'Don't think so,' came the reply, 'I saw them ride away – first three before the bullets hit us, an' then another three whilst I was here with your pa.'

Dan was staring at the burning house. 'Nothin' we can do there,' he muttered. 'We'll hev to use the stable tonight, it's the only building left.'

They carried Bill Collins inside the stable, lit the lamp and after washing the wound, bound it up carefully. Jack forced a drink between his father's lips and a few moments later his eyes flickered open, but it was about ten minutes before things began to focus in his mind and he started to look around.

A look of surprise crossed his face. His eyes widened disbelievingly. 'Jack! Howard! It can't be!' he whispered. 'Dan! Clint! You too!'

'All right, pa, take it easy,' said Jack quietly. 'It's us, we're back.'

'Everythin' will be all right now,' said Howard comfortingly.

When Bill Collins felt sufficiently recovered he told them the story of his troubles. 'So you see,' he continued, 'this is the end, I'll hev to sell out. I won't git the same offer from Pete Young now.'

'He made an offer today,' muttered Dan, thoughtfully, 'which you refused an' then your house is burnt down an' the last two cowhands killed. Could be he's tryin' to force your hand.'

'I don't think so,' said Bill. 'I was suspicious of them when they first came, but I can't connect anythin' with them. Besides, if he intended to do this, why bother to make an offer?'

'A blind,' replied Dan. 'Same as these other raids could be. No one has been hit as hard as you.'

'I've never liked the Youngs from the time they arrived,' grunted Clint.

'I think we'll pay them a visit tomorrow,' said Dan, 'but first I've got to find out who is really Sheriff of Red Springs.'

When the two men rode into Red Springs

the next morning, their arrival did not go unobserved, and by the time they approached the sheriff's office, there was a fair-sized crowd along the sidewalks. As he pulled to a halt, Dan's eyes took in the details of the stranger who leaned on the rail outside the sheriff's office. The tin star pinned to his brown shirt told Dan that this was the man he was looking for, but most of all he noted the smooth butt of the Colt which hung low on the man's hips, and Dan knew he was facing a man who was used to handling the gun. Dan swung from his horse and threw the reins to Clint, who knew that was an indication that Dan wanted him to remain on his horse and not interfere.

'Howdy, sheriff,' greeted Dan, as he stood in the roadway facing the stranger.

The man grinned and straightened himself. 'Glad you recognise the fact,' he said. 'You ride in here with Schofield an' wear a tin star, I figure you must be McCoy.' Dan nodded his agreement. 'Hev you come to hand in the badge?'

'No,' replied Dan sharply. 'Come to git yours.'

The man laughed. 'Now thet isn't possible. I was put in here as sheriff by these townsfolk an' I aim to keep it thet way.'

'From what I hear they were bamboozled into electing you,' snapped Dan. 'Persuaded by slick-talking by a certain Pete Young. Could be he brought you here fer the job.'

The man's eyes narrowed, he moved slowly off the sidewalk. Dan's brain pounded as he watched him carefully, trying to think where he had seen him before.

'I was jest passin' through an'….'

His words were cut short by Dan, who suddenly recognised him.

'I'll not hev a notorious gunman as Sheriff of my town. Runnin' things so that Pete Young can rule the territory.' His voice lashed the words from his throat.

The man laughed. 'You're out of your mind,' he shouted.

'Am I?' snarled Dan. 'I spent some time in Wyoming a few years ago and I know…'

The initial movement of the man's hand had been almost imperceptible and too late Dan realised he would be beaten to the draw by a shorter reach. He moved swiftly to one side, pulling his gun from its holster, his words drowned by the roar of the stranger's Colt. The bullet grazed his arm as he squeezed the trigger, but his movement deflected his aim and the bullet crashed into

174

the man's shoulder as his gun roared again, but a fraction of a second too late. The force of Dan's bullet had spun him sideways and his shot went high. Dan recovered his balance quickly and as he crouched his gun roared again and again, sending lead crashing into the stranger's chest.

He staggered backwards against the sidewalk, and as his knees buckled he pitched sideways, to sprawl lifeless in the dust.

Dan straightened himself slowly, staring at the silent figure. Suddenly, he was brought back to reality, when everyone in the crowd who had been silent from the first moment of the encounter, all started to talk and shout at once. Clint was by his side grasping his arm.

'You all right?' he asked.

Dan nodded.

'You knew him?' queried Clint.

'One of the slickest gun-men thet ever rode the State of Wyoming,' answered Dan. 'Butch Evans.'

Dan glanced round at the crowd without a word, and as he walked into the sheriff's office, he knew he had re-established himself as the rightful lawman of Red Springs.

A few minutes later Dan and Clint mounted their horses and left Red Springs at a brisk trot. When they reached the Circle C they found Bill Collins and his sons eager to ride to the Bar X.

As they neared the ranch, Dan noted a number of cowboys doing various jobs close to the ranch-house, and as they rode nearer the building, he realised if any trouble started they would be caught in a deadly crossfire.

Dan frowned. It looked as if they had been expected and yet how would the Youngs have known they were even in the district, unless someone had ridden from town? As they pulled to a halt in front of the veranda, a man appeared round the end of the buildings.

'Howdy,' he greeted pleasantly.

Dan saw him stare at the star on his shirt. 'Surprised to see thet?' asked Dan with a smile.

'Yeah,' answered the cowboy.

'I'm Dan McCoy, Sheriff of Red Springs,' exclaimed Dan. 'Thet hombre thet the Youngs helped to put in came to a bad end; you hadn't heard about it?'

'Nope,' the man shook his head. 'If it's the Youngs you want to see,' he went on, 'I'm afraid you're out of luck. They've gone south, buyin' cattle.'

'Too bad,' answered Dan. 'When do you expect them back?'

'They didn't say,' came the reply. 'Mart Webster's the name, an' they left me in charge.' He turned to Bill Collins. 'They told me to tell you they were still interested in buying the Circle C, at half the price Pete offered yesterday.'

'What!' gasped Collins, 'thet's a give-away price!'

'Wal, you couldn't expect any more now,' replied Webster.

'Why not?' asked Dan sharply. 'Nothing's changed to alter the price has it?'

'Wal, I… Pete said,' Mart stuttered, 'wal, the offer was only open up to midnight.'

Dan eyed the man suspiciously. Things weren't adding up correctly. He saw Bill Collins' look of amazement at Webster's last statement and, realizing he was going to remark about it, he spoke quickly.

'Wal, if the Youngs are away, there's nothing to hang around here fer,' he said. 'I'll pay them a call later.' He nodded to Webster and pulled his horse round quickly, knowing the others would follow suit. They rode away at a fast trot, but once out of sight of the ranch Dan pulled to a halt.

'Pete Young said nothin' about the offer

being open until midnight,' stormed Bill Collins, as he pulled alongside Dan. 'I was goin' to challenge Webster about it, but you suddenly rode out.'

'I thought you were,' replied Dan, 'but I didn't want Webster to know we were suspicious of his statement. I think he began to realise he'd said too much when he said you couldn't expect more than half price now – he obviously knew about the fire; but how?' Dan looked thoughtful. 'He said that no one had been out from town, besides, if they had, then he'd hev known about me an' his surprise seemed genuine enough.'

'There's one way he could hev known about the fire,' pointed out Howard, 'an' thet's if the Youngs caused it!'

'There's somethin' peculiar about the whole set-up,' said Dan thoughtfully. 'I think I'll pay the Bar X another visit, this evening!'

'An' when you do,' said Bill, 'pay attention to Barbara's old room. The blinds are up at the windows so you can't see in, but I'm sure I heard someone in there.'

Chapter Twelve

Dan left his horse some distance from the Bar X and moved swiftly but quietly through the darkness towards the house. As he expected, with the Youngs away, no light shone from the building, but a short distance away the bunk-house was well lit. He had insisted on coming alone, telling the Collins brothers that they deserved a night in town, and that one man would have a better chance of looking round the Bar X.

Dan, listening intently, waited beside the veranda for a few moments, but the only sound came from the bunk-house. He slipped quietly to the front door and, finding it unlocked, stepped quickly inside. He paused, listening, but the house was quiet. Hurrying quickly to the room which he knew had been Barbara's, he was glad to find the door open. Once inside he struck a match, sending shadows dancing round the walls. He lit a lamp which stood on a table and examined the room carefully. It was obvious that it had been occupied recently, but by whom he could not tell. Feeling frustrated he moved towards the door, when the edge of a piece of material sticking out from under the dressing table, caught his eye. He picked it up and as he held it nearer the light, he gasped with surprise.

'Barbara's shawl!' he whispered. 'But how did it get here?' His brain pounded with all sorts of possibilities.

It was essential that no one should know he had been here: he must get back to the Circle C as quickly as possible. He blew out the light, stepped out of the room and hurried to the front door. Opening it quietly, he stepped swiftly outside, closing the door silently behind him as he flattened himself against it, glancing in both directions.

Suddenly he stiffened. The sound of boots on the hard ground reached his ears. Someone was coming towards the house from the direction of the bunk-house. The figure of a cowboy gradually emerged from the darkness. Dan tensed himself, hoping the man would walk straight past, but he turned and walked up the steps leading on to the veranda in front of the door. As the man moved forward, Dan leaped, crashing his fist into the man's jaw. He staggered backwards, falling down the steps into an inert heap on the ground. Dan jumped over him and ran in the direction of his horse. He swung into the saddle, but before putting the horse into a fast gallop he listened, his head inclined towards the Bar X, but there was no sound of alarm.

Reaching the Circle C, Dan hurried to the stable.

'Look at this!' he called, holding out the shawl to Bill Collins.

'Thet's Barbara's,' said Bill in amazement. 'Where did you git it?'

'I found it in Barbara's old room,' replied Dan.

'What!' Bill stared incredulously at Dan. 'But she never hed any of her things there since she married you.'

'I thought not,' said Dan. 'You sure she never left this when she's been visitin' you.'

'Certain,' answered Bill.

Dan looked thoughtful, a worried frown creased his brow. 'You know what this means,' he said quietly.

'Wal, I can't figure out how it came...' Bill stopped, and stared hard at Dan, a look of amazement crossing his face. 'You don't mean...' he gasped. 'The Youngs are really the Browns!'

Dan nodded.

'But how…' started Bill.

'It could figure you know,' said Dan. 'I've been doin' some thinkin' as I rode back here. The Browns hear of the killin' of Wes an' swear revenge. Lee Brown comes here to kill me. He took the precaution, however, of kidnapping Babs in case I killed him. By sendin' her to his brothers he hoped thet I would follow, an' fall into their hands.' He paused thoughtfully. 'When I got shot in the Wichitas,' he continued, 'it must hev been by someone who recognized me – but thet bit I can't figure out – and was in with the Browns. Thinkin' me dead, they come to Red Springs, falsely claim the Bar X, run Clint out of town an' nearly ruin you.'

'It's fantastic,' said Collins.

'Maybe,' replied Dan, 'but possible.'

'How did they git the story of the Bar X?' asked Bill.

'Thet's what puzzles me,' said Dan, rubbing his chin thoughtfully. Suddenly he snapped his fingers. 'I've got it. The person that shot me must hev known the story, an' thet can only hev been one of the Pickering outfit; remember, two of them were never caught.'

'Could be,' agreed Collins.

'An' I'll bet the Browns are not away

buyin' cattle, but somewhere close at hand.'

'They must hev hung around after the raid last night an' seen you ride in,' said Collins excitedly.

'But they wouldn't know me as McCoy,' pointed out Dan.

'No, but they'd recognise you as workin' with them in Oklahoma; this hombre from the Pickering outfit must hev been with them an' he would know you as McCoy.'

Dan slapped his thigh. 'You're right, Bill. They'd expect us at the Bar X, an' knowin' I would recognise them, they've gone into hidin'.'

'Taking Barbara with them,' added Bill.

'It all adds up,' mused Dan. 'An' if they've still got Barbara we've got to move carefully.' He paused thoughtfully. 'What time you expectin' the boys back?'

'Any time,' replied Collins.

As the darkness covered the Texas countryside, Jack and Howard Collins, accompanied by Clint Schofield, rode at a steady trot towards Red Springs. They would have preferred to have been with Dan on his way to the Bar X, but he had insisted on going alone.

There were few people about on the main

street as they pulled up in front of the saloon.

'If you don't mind boys, I won't come,' said Clint. 'There'll be a few things to see to in the office an' it will help Dan if I git them cleared up. Call fer me when you're ready.'

'All right, Clint,' said Jack. 'We won't be long.'

Clint turned his horse across the street, whilst Howard and Jack went into the saloon, where they pushed their way to the bar and ordered drinks, unaware that their arrival had been noted by three men sitting at a table close to the door.

Mart Webster glanced at his two companions as the Collins brothers reached the bar. 'Looks as if we're goin' to deal with those two hombres sooner than expected,' he grinned. Half an hour passed, during which time he watched the brothers carefully. 'Reckon we'd better be gettin' outside,' he said.

The three men left the table and pushed through the batwings into the darkness of the main street. They moved down the sidewalk a little way from the entrance to the saloon and eased the guns in their holsters.

Five minutes later the batwings squeaked open and Jack and Howard crossed the sidewalk and headed for the sheriff's office across the street. Suddenly the darkness was split by a flash as a rifle roared in front of them. They heard a yell behind them as they dived into the dust and rolled over and over. Once again the rifle crashed and the immediate silence was broken by the sound of feet running along the wooden sidewalk. The rifle spoke again and the footsteps faltered, tried to run again, stopped, scraped along wood, and were followed by a bump, then silence.

The Collins brothers pushed themselves to their feet, wondering what all the shooting had been about. They looked up and saw Clint Schofield, a rifle in his hand, move out from the shadows of the sidewalk opposite the saloon. Cowboys poured out of the saloon.

'You all right?' asked Clint, when he reached the brothers.

'Yes thanks,' replied Jack, slapping the dust from his clothes. 'What's it all about?'

'Webster an' two of the men from the Bar X tried to get you,' answered Clint.

'How did you git on to them?' queried Howard curiously.

'I changed my mind about thet drink,' explained Clint, 'but I happened to stop an' look over the batwings. I saw those three sitting near the door. Webster was talking to the two men and nodding in your direction. I didn't like the look on his face an' so I thought I'd keep watch out here – the saloon was too crowded for him to try anythin' in there.'

'Good job fer us you felt thirsty,' observed Jack with a grin. 'C'm on, let's git back to the Circle C.'

They mounted their horses and left Red Springs at a fast trot, and were soon at the Circle C, where they were surprised to learn of Dan's discovery.

'Seems they're bent on gettin' everyone who had anythin' to do in the Wes Brown affair,' said Jack. 'An' they'd hev got us tonight if it hadn't been fer Clint.' He went on to relate what had happened in Red Springs.

'They're stepping up their war,' said Dan when Jack finished his story. 'We must move carefully to find out where they've got Barbara. It's my hunch the Browns will return to the Bar X at some time, especially when they hear of Clint's work tonight, so if Jack and Howard keep watch on the place, we might git a lead on them.'

Early the following morning Jack and Howard took up a position near the Bar X, but already Wally was riding to a pre-arranged meeting with the Browns on the Brazos River, close to their hideout.

Ed Brown was waiting when Wally rode up.

'Everythin' all right?' asked Ed, noting Wally's grave face as he swung from the saddle.

'Like hell it is,' snapped Wally. 'Mart an' two of the boys were killed in Red Springs last night.'

'What!' gasped Brown. 'How did it happen?'

'Apparently they went gunning the Collins boys, but Schofield hed the drop on them,' answered Wally testily.

'Fools!' snarled Brown from between clenched teeth. 'Careless fools! We can't afford to make mistakes.'

'Thet's not all,' went on Wally. 'Someone was prowling round the ranch last night.'

Ed frowned. 'Who was it?' he asked, annoyance toning his voice.

'Don't know,' replied Wally. 'One of the boys was jumped, laid out before he got a sight of who it was.'

Ed Brown cursed loudly. 'Things were goin' our way, now they're turning for the worse,' he said. 'We still hev Mrs McCoy if things get to hot. Keep an eye on things at the ranch, Wally. Nick an' I will come in this afternoon, after we've worked somethin' out. I'd hoped to lie low without revealin' our identity to McCoy fer a while, but maybe it would be better to come out into the open now.'

Chapter Thirteen

It was mid-afternoon when Jack Collins saw three figures riding towards the Bar X, along the bank of river. He pointed them out to Howard and the two men watched the riders carefully as they approached the ranch.

'The Browns!' whispered Jack, as the men came near enough to be recognised. 'Never expected them to show up so soon.'

'Dan was right,' said Howard, 'I remember thet third hombre – used to ride with the Pickerings, name of Burgess.'

'Wonder what they've done with Babs?' said Jack grimly.

They watched the three men dismount and, together with Wally, enter the house. Ten minutes later Burgess and Wally hurried out and called to six cowboys. In a few minutes they were all mounted and milling around in front of the house. The Brown brothers emerged, Nick swung into the saddle and led the band of men away from the Bar X at a fast gallop. Ed Brown watched them for a moment before mounting his horse and riding towards the river.

'They're headin' fer the Circle C!' Alarm showed in Howard's voice as he watched the nine riders turn their horses towards his father's ranch. He glanced at the diminishing figure of Ed Brown. 'What about him?' he asked.

'We should follow him,' replied Jack, 'but they'll be outnumbered at the Circle C if we don't go. I reckon Babs will be all right; Brown's sure to want to see how things go.'

The two men hurried to the horses, swung into the saddles and put them into a fast gallop, but Nick Brown and his gang had already got a good start.

Bill Collins, assisted by Dan, Clint and his foreman, were at work on the erection of the new ranch-house when they heard the thunder of galloping horses. Looking up in alarm, Bill Collins was the first to see the riders as they breasted a slight hill on the trail.

'Nine of them!' he yelled.

'Nick Brown at the head!' shouted Clint.

'This is trouble with a capital T,' called Dan, watching the fast, determined approach of the riders. He sized up the situation quickly. 'Stay inside here,' he shouted, 'these

190

four half-built walls will give us good cover.'

The four men lined themselves along the wall facing the oncoming horses. It looked as if Nick Brown was determined to ride right through, but on his signal, his men opened fire some distance from the new erection. Bullets thundered harmlessly into the wood and immediately Dan and his friends opened fire, causing the riders to pull to a halt and scatter, seeking the shelter of fences, wagons, and the stables. Spasmodic firing from both sides shattered the Texas air, but it had no effect on either side.

Dan realised that Brown could keep them pinned down all day and move in on them under cover of darkness, but Nick was determined not to wait that long, as he felt that darkness would provide the trapped men with the cover necessary to escape. He signalled to his men, leaped to his feet, and dived for shelter, whilst his companions kept up a covering fire. Gradually the gang spread themselves round the building and, on Nick's signal, poured a withering fire towards the trapped men. Suddenly the firing stopped.

'McCoy!' shouted Nick, 'or should it be Ferguson? You remember Wes Brown? Wal...'

'I know,' yelled Dan, interrupting Nick. 'You're his brother. I figured things out when I found my wife's shawl at the Bar X. Where is she now?'

'Wouldn't you like to know?' laughed Nick harshly.

'If you've harmed her I'll...' Dan's threat was cut short.

'You'll do nothin',' yelled Brown. "Cos you haven't got a chance penned up in there. Tell you what, you come out of there an' I'll see she goes free!'

Dan's brain pounded. Barbara was all right. But could he trust these outlaws? Bill Collins saw Dan battling with the predicament in which he was placed.

'Dan, don't do it,' he called softly. 'You can't trust them. We'll git out of here all right.'

'What about my friends here?' shouted Dan.

'Thet'll be up to Ed,' replied Nick.

'Is he there?' called Dan.

'He's keepin' your wife company!' laughed Nick.

Collins raised his rifle and fired in the direction of the voice. 'There's your answer,' he shouted. 'McCoy stays here, an' if you want him you'll hev to git rid of us first.'

A volley of shots from all sides whined around the walls. The four men kept careful watch from each side of the half-built house and whenever they saw a movement they returned the fire. As one of the outlaws tried to sneak in closer, Bill Collins' rifle crashed and with a yell the man straightened, grasping at his shoulder. The rifle spoke again and this time the outlaw jerked upright and pitched forward on to his face.

'One less,' called Bill.

At that moment a shot rang out above them and as Dan whirled he saw Bill Collins' foreman spin round and slump against the wall. Dan's rifle came up quickly and before the man, who had climbed on to the roof of the stable, could take aim at anybody else, he fired. The outlaw threw up his arms and pitched headlong from the roof.

The firing gradually died away and both sides took stock of the situation. Suddenly the silence was shattered by the crack of a rifle. The men behind the wooden walls automatically crouched, then slowly straightened, staring at each other in amazement when they realised no bullet had thudded into the wood nor whined overhead. The rifle crashed again and almost at the same another fired. Dan peered cautiously out and

193

gasped when he saw two still forms laid a short distance from the half-finished house.

'They must hev been trying to sneak in on us,' he said. 'But who shot them?'

'Suddenly a shot rang out, but this time further to the right. It was followed by a yell as a man stumbled into view. Dan did not hesitate. He drew his Colt and dropped the man as he tried to run for his horse. A burst of firing broke out to the left and Clint and Bill ran over to Dan in time to see four men, including Nick Brown, move from cover in a crouching run. They kept close to a fence, using every available protection, as they ran towards their horses. A rifle crashed and one of the men faltered in his step, tried to carry on, and then fell on to his knees before sprawling on his face in the dust. Clint brought his rifle to his shoulder, following the running figures carefully until an opportunity presented itself, then he squeezed the trigger gently. His shot stopped the first man dead in his tracks, his knees buckled and he fell in a heap on the floor. His two companions leaped over the body, found the shelter of a wagon and crawled slowly forward, until they were only a few yards from their horses. They paused, gulping air into their aching lungs. Nick Brown, his face black with anger, cursed loudly at the turn of events. He eased himself up and loosed off six shots towards the house. At almost the same moment as he fired the last shot he leaped to his feet and, followed by the other outlaw, raced to his horse.

When Dan saw the two men run for their horses, his rifle was quickly at his shoulder, but he found his aim on Brown was obscured by the other man. A rifle crashed beside him and he saw the man stumble and fall forward, but before Dan could fire, Brown had reached the horses. He turned his mount quickly so that it shielded him, and with one foot in the stirrup, he held on to the saddle, letting the horse carry him out of range of the rifles, before swinging into the saddle and urging the animal into an earth-pounding gallop.

A yell broke the concentration of the men inside the house, and they ran through the half-finished doorway to greet their rescuers.

'Jack! Howard!' shouted Bill as he raced forward to meet his sons, who were running towards the house from different directions. 'We wondered who it was,' he said, clapping them on their backs. 'Mighty glad to see you.'

'Clint,' yelled Dan, as he raced from the

house towards the horses, 'stay with Bill, Brown'll lead me to Barbara!' He hurled himself into the saddle and kicked the horse into a gallop in the direction taken by Brown.

Seeing their brother-in-law running for his horse, Jack and Howard turned to their father. 'We'll bring Barbara back,' said Jack. They ran to their mounts and galloped after Dan.

'Barbara must be somewhere down the Brazos,' shouted Howard. 'Ed Brown headed thet way. But as we thought you might be in a fix we followed Nick instead.'

Dan nodded and the three men flattened themselves in the saddles, calling to their powerful animals for greater effort. After two miles of fast riding, they came in sight of Nick Brown, who, glancing over his shoulder, saw them and lashed his horse into a harder run.

Earth flew as the horses pounded over the ground, but the distance between Nick Brown and his pursuers did not shorten.

'We've got him cornered between that thorn land and the river,' shouted Jack as they rode into a hollow.

They topped the rise and pulled hard on the reins, staring in amazement at the empty countryside. Nick Brown had disappeared!

'It's impossible,' gasped Howard, 'he must be somewhere.'

'Can't get through that thorn,' said Jack.

'Thet leaves the river,' added Dan.

'Impossible, the way it runs here just before the rapids,' pointed out Jack.

'Wal, c'm on, let's take a look round,' said Dan, disappointedly pushing his horse forward.

The three men rode slowly towards the river, searching everywhere for some place that Brown could be hiding. They reached the edge of the river, but still there was no sign of the outlaw. Swinging out of the saddles they tied their horses to a tree.

'It's a mystery,' said Dan, 'but spread out along the river an' see if we can pick up a clue.'

Ten minutes went by without a sign. Dan and Howard had come together again, but Jack had moved into the thorn-covered area until it became so thick that it impeded his progress. He was close to the water and about to turn back and rejoin Dan and his brother, when something struck him as peculiar about the river at this point. Close to the bank it was not flowing as fast as in midstream and looked gentler and much shallower. He edged a little further along

197

the bank and gasped with surprise when he saw hoof marks on the edge of the bank. He yelled for Dan, and a few moments later they crashed their way through thorn bushes to reach him.

'He's been here!' he said excitedly, pointing to the tell-tale marks.

'Looks as if he went into the water,' said Dan, who looked across the river. A puzzled frown creased his forehead. 'But where did he go?'

Suddenly Howard jumped into the river close to the bank side. Surprised by his action, Dan and Jack gasped when they saw that the water only came up to his knees.

'Seems to be a shelf running parallel with the bank,' he said. 'Brown must have used it. The bank steepens further along, maybe there's some hiding place.'

Dan and Jack jumped down beside him and the three men moved forward slowly.

They had gone about thirty yards, when a Colt crashed above the roar of the river. The bullet whined unpleasantly close to their heads and each man froze in his tracks.

'There he is,' pointed out Dan, indicating Nick Brown, who peered from behind a rock on the bank side. He loosed off a shot which ricocheted off the rock into the water.

'Must be a cutting there,' he said, 'an' it's my guess they've got Barbara in there.'

'Hold off, McCoy,' a voice yelled. 'This is Ed Brown. We...'

'I'm coming gunnin' fer you,' yelled Dan.

'Try thet an' your wife gets it,' answered Brown viciously. 'You'd better throw in your hand, we hold the trump card.'

'What do you want me to do?' Dan shouted.

'Jest come forward gentle like, on your own, and then we'll work from there,' called Brown.

Dan thought for a moment. 'All right, Brown, I'll come, but you must promise to let my wife go unharmed,' he added.

'Sure,' returned Brown.

'You're not goin,' Dan,' pleaded Jack urgently. 'Don't trust those coyotes. As soon as you're out there, they'll shoot you down.'

'I know,' said Dan, 'but it's a risk I've got to take, if we're to git Barbara out of there. I'm goin' to take a dive into the river an' come out on the bank below them. When I go in, give them all the fire you've got, an' keep them occupied – I don't want them to see me come up.'

'What about your gun? It will be wet,' said Howard.

199

'I've got a knife,' replied Dan grimly.

Any further conversation was cut short by Brown.

'Are you comin'?' he yelled. 'We can't wait all day.'

'I'm comin' now,' answered Dan, and started to move along the ledges towards the Brown brothers.

'A sitting duck,' laughed Nick harshly, and raised his Colt.

'Hold it,' snapped Ed. 'He's mine.'

Dan, knowing that a bullet might fly in his direction at any moment, stumbled and hurled himself into the river. With a yell, Nick loosed off two shots which hit water close to Dan. At the same moment Jack and Howard opened fire, sending a fusillade of shots at the Browns, forcing them to keep behind cover. Dan knew he would be exposed to the guns of the Brown brothers as he swept past the end of the cutting, so he swam further away from the bank, before letting the swirling waters take charge and sweep him down-stream.

Ed watched the river closely and when he saw Dan tumbling and twisting in the foaming water, he raised his Colt and fired. As the bullet spanged the water close to Dan's face, he took a deep breath, flung up his arms, and plunged beneath the surface.

'Got him!' yelled Ed triumphantly, and the Brown bothers turned their attention to Jack and Howard.

'We're getting' your sister and comin' out,' shouted Ed. 'Don't try anything or she'll git a bullet!'

Under the water, Dan let it carry him until his lungs were bursting for want of air. As he broke the surface he glanced anxiously towards the cutting in the bank-side. Nick Brown was watching for any movement on the part of the Collins brothers, but Ed was nowhere to be seen. Dan's thoughts raced. Ed must have gone for Barbara, there was not a moment to lose. He struck out strongly, and on reaching the steep, rocky bank, he pulled himself out of the water, only to find that there was no way along the bank-side.

He glanced upwards and saw there was a narrow ledge halfway up the rocky face, which offered his only chance of working his way towards the Browns. Making use of every hold, he climbed the rock face to the ledge, which widened as it neared the cutting.

Realising that if Nick Brown turned round he would be seen, he moved swiftly forward to the point where the rock face turned into the cutting, putting himself in a commanding position above the Browns.

A movement attracted his attention and he pressed himself back against the rock face as Ed Brown appeared, pushing Barbara in front of him. Her eyes were red and swollen, tears streamed down her face, and Dan knew Ed Brown had told her he had killed him. She stumbled as Brown pushed her forward roughly. Dan found it hard to control himself, but he knew with only a knife to face two men with guns, he must seize the right opportunity. The moment, however, was forced upon him. As Ed pushed Barbara close to the water's edge, Nick turned to greet them. The triumphant leer on his face froze when he saw Dan on the rock face above them. The surprise shocked him and as he leaped to his feet to bring his Colt on Dan, he exposed himself to the gun of Howard Collins and before he could fire, a bullet thudded into his back, sending him crashing to the ground.

Startled, Ed hesitated, wondering what was happening and then, seeing Dan, he leaped to grab Barbara, but that fraction's hesitation brought him death. As he jumped forward, Dan flung his knife, and saw it plunge deep into Ed's side. The man stopped as if he had run into a wall and then in one last effort his arm encircled Barbara, swinging her round in front of him. She fought, trying to get out of his grip. His Colt roared and the bullet hit the rock face close to Dan's head, sending splinters of rock cutting his face. The strength suddenly drained from Ed and before he could fire again his knees buckled, his arm dropped and the gun fell on to the rocks. His hold relaxed and, when Barbara pushed harder to free herself, Ed staggered backwards, lost his balance and fell into the river. The swirling waters grasped him, pulled him under, tossed him to the surface again and from the cliff Dan saw the body hurled towards the rapids.

Dan turned his attention to Barbara, and after picking his way down the rock face he soon held his sobbing wife in his arms.

'Dan I never thought I'd see you again,' she cried.

'It's all over now,' comforted Dan. 'The Browns are finished, so maybe we'll git back to normal an' git the ranch organised.'